**'Are we going t**
**when you move**
**breathlessly.**

Gavin's brain shut down. 'Aw, hell.'
Reminded of his plan, he shoved himself
away from her. How did that saying go? You
won't buy the cow if the milk is free? Not
that he liked comparing himself to a cow. A
bull, maybe...

'Sara, if this is going to work, you're going to
have to stop making it so easy on me.'

'Me? What about you? You're the one who
started the kissing.'

'Yeah. But you didn't have to go all soft and
hungry on me.'

'I'm not going to let you blame me for this,
Gavin! You're the one who climbed into bed
with me.'

'But I'm not the one who tried to crawl on top
of you in the middle of the night.'

She sucked in so much air, she choked. 'I
would *never*...!'

Nodding, he said, 'Yes, you would. *You did.*'
Then he added in a low voice before she
could get too worked up, 'But I didn't mind
at all.'

Dear Reader,

When I was six years old, I won a drawing contest in the city newspaper. The prize was a complete Worldbook Encyclopaedia set. (And lucky for me, a rubber finger puppet!) My parents made me a deal. I'd give them the encyclopaedias until I graduated, and they'd buy me anything I wanted. I wanted a baby pig.

At a nearby farm we found the most adorable little spotted piglets running around playing. But there was one especially homely pig, just sort of grey, sort of fat, sort of shy. I chose him. And named him after Monnie, my grandma.

He got fatter and uglier as time went by, and finally I gave him to a local farmer who promised to keep him as a stud pig. Monnie was happy until the day he died.

I've always loved animals—the tail-less cat, the bird with a broken wing, the snake a neighbour wanted to kill, the dog who shed too much. Every animal I've come into contact with has added something to my life.

This story is about a woman who loves pets just as much as I do—especially the dysfunctional or ugly ones.

Of course she needs a man who'll love them as well, so I found him for her.

I hope you enjoy *Say Yes!*

Lori Foster

P.S. You can write to Lori at PO Box 854, Ross OH 45061, USA, or send an e-mail to lorifoster@poboxes.com

# SAY YES

by

# Lori Foster

MILLS & BOON®

*All the characters in this book have no existence outside the imagination
of the author, and have no relation whatsoever to anyone bearing the
same name or names. They are not even distantly inspired by any
individual known or unknown to the author, and all the incidents are
pure invention.*

*First published in Great Britain 2001
by Harlequin Mills & Boon Limited,
Eton House, 18-24 Paradise Road, Richmond, Surrey TW9 1SR*

© Lori Foster 2000

ISBN 0 263 82817 4

*21-1001*

*Printed and bound in Spain
by Litografia Rosés S.A., Barcelona*

To my computer-guru buddy and good friend
Jen Sokoloski. Without you, Jen, my computer and all
that goes with it would likely still be a mystery. <g>
Thank you for all your help.

And to Linda Keller, my best friend.
Thank you so much for listening, talking,
sharing, giving—for being you.

# 1

IT WAS THE LOUD, SHRILL scream of rage that drew Gavin Blake's attention, along with the frantic shrieks that followed. Gavin stared down the middle of the narrow street, blinking hard to make certain he wasn't hallucinating. But no. There was his usually calm, very friendly neighbor Sara Simmons, her dark curly hair bouncing out behind her as she ran hell-bent after Karen, his used-to-be girlfriend. He hadn't seen Karen in months, not since their breakup, and the sight of her now wasn't what fascinated him. No, it was gentle, sweet, *passive* Sara—who at the moment held a rake which she wielded with all the force and efficiency of a massive war club. And each time she swung it, punctuating her efforts with low, threatening growls, Karen wailed in fear.

A disbelieving smile twitched on his mouth as he heard Sara issue a rather lurid, improbable threat. So far as Gavin could tell, Sara hadn't even touched Karen yet, but it was a close thing.

Karen's shirt was open, but her efforts were all centered on escaping the woman bent on retribution, not on covering her half-naked chest. As they neared the entrance to the garage where Gavin stood, he tried to get himself out of the way. But Karen made eye contact, and evidently, even though they were no longer involved, she decided he might be her savior.

Hah! Sara behaved very much like a woman scorned—or a woman who had caught her fiancé intimately involved with another woman. And knowing Karen as he did, that assumption wasn't unrealistic. He'd learned some time ago that Karen would never be a faithful, devoted, loving partner. Which was why he'd ended the relationship and sent her on her way months ago.

But as the two women ran straight for him and he saw the fury—and the hurt—in Sara's eyes, Gavin knew for a certainty Karen had been up to her old tricks. He decided to stay out of the matter and let Sara do her worst, knowing she wouldn't actually hurt Karen. But the women had other ideas.

They tried to use him as a maypole.

He dropped the file he'd been holding and saw the approved plans for another subdivision scatter across the garage floor. He struggled to maintain his balance with Karen trying to shield herself behind him and Sara trying to go straight through him. He bent to retrieve a floor plan being mangled under furious feminine feet and was promptly shoved away and onto his backside. Having just come from the office, he was unfortunately wearing dress pants. He started to grumble, but then Karen made a dive for the house, and Sara followed, climbing right over the top of him.

There was another loud screech, and Gavin couldn't help but grin. He'd known since first meeting Sara that she was a passionate little thing, filled with energy and an abundance of emotion. But this was the first time he'd seen that emotion really set free. The jerk she'd planned to marry would never have made her happy. Gavin supposed, in a way, he owed Karen his thanks for showing Sara just how big a jerk Ted really was.

Then he heard the sound of breaking glass and decided he'd have to intervene after all. Knowing Sara, and he'd come to know her very well since she'd moved into one of the houses he built, she'd hate her loss of control once she calmed down.

He wondered briefly if she'd allow him to console her.

Coming up behind Sara, he was just in time to

duck the rake as she took another swipe at the cowered, screeching Karen. Gavin snatched it out of her hands, and when she rounded on him, he pulled her close in a careful bear hug. "Just calm down, honey."

He tried to keep the satisfaction and good humor out of his tone. Little by little, the enormity of the situation was sinking in, and he was starting to feel damn good. He'd now see the end of Sara's fiancé—and without a guilty conscience. He'd held back, keeping his personal interest to himself, unwilling to involve himself in a set relationship, even though he knew the relationship was doomed. Sara was much too good for Ted, she just hadn't seemed to realize it.

But with these new crimes against him, Sara would surely send Ted packing. Finally they would both be free of ties, and he'd be able to pursue her the way he wanted to.

Sara growled, and he had to admit, the menacing sound was very effective. "Let me go, Gavin."

*No way.* She felt damn good in his arms, too good. He looked down at her rigid expression, her bright eyes, and had to fight to keep from kissing her. This was the first time he'd ever been able to actually hold her, and he liked it—a lot. She growled again and he saw that slightly crooked front tooth, the one that always taunted him, made him want to touch it with his tongue. He tightened his hold just a bit more, relishing the feel of her small body tucked up against his, and breathed in her gentle fragrance. Sara always smelled of sunshine and softness and woman. He lowered his mouth to her ear.

''I think you've made your point, honey. Karen understands the error of her ways.''

She struggled in his arms. ''You don't know what they... They were in my *house*, in my bed!''

He did know. The house meant everything to Sara, but very little to Ted. In fact, Sara had bought the place herself, no small feat for a woman alone with a moderate income. And not a day went by that she didn't tell him what a wonderful job he'd done building that house. She made him feel as if he'd given her the moon.

''It won't happen again, Sara. I promise.''

He had a hell of a time controlling his elation. And when Sara peeked up at him with energy and emotion blazing in her blue eyes, he couldn't help himself. He smiled.

Very slowly she looked around. A lamp lay broken on the floor and Gavin saw her wince. When her gaze landed on the shattered picture, she closed her eyes as if in pain. Color flooded her smooth cheeks.

Behind him, he heard the sounds of Karen slinking away. No doubt she planned to make a strategic retreat. Gavin ignored her. In the three months she'd been gone, he hadn't missed her once. "Sara? Are you okay now?"

"Let—me—go."

Cautiously, making certain she wouldn't bolt after Karen again, Gavin lowered his arms. She stood there, her eyes still closed, her cheeks pulsing with heat. She said in a strangled whisper, "I'm sorry."

Gavin touched her cheek, swamped with tenderness and a real healthy dose of desire. "Hey, don't worry about it. After a boring day in the office, I needed a little excitement."

She drew in a long, slow breath, then opened her eyes, but didn't look at him. Instead she surveyed the damage. "I didn't mean to break anything."

"Karen would probably disagree."

Her gaze shot to his face and her hands curled into fists. "I don't want her anywhere near me ever again."

She was such a ferocious, impassioned little thing when duly provoked. "Don't worry. I think

Karen has learned her lesson. Besides, I wasn't the one who invited her here.''

She scowled. "No. Ted apparently did."

"What will you do?" He was very curious, but he held no sympathy for Ted. In fact, he wanted to rub his hands in glee over Ted's folly. The idiot.

Sara lifted her chin, then slowly stepped around the broken glass on the floor. "I'll take care of Ted." Gavin watched her stiff posture as she walked away, and he wondered if he should accompany her home so she wouldn't have to face Ted alone. Then he thought better of it.

Ted didn't stand a chance.

Besides, Sara was private, with a streak of dignity and pride a mile wide. She wouldn't want an audience when she gave Ted the boot. He knew Sara—not as well as he'd like to, but probably better than Ted would ever know her. At least he knew enough to realize how important old-fashioned values were to her. Possibly because they were important to him as well.

She'd talk to Ted, listen to his lame excuses, then toss him out on his miserable can. She'd be hurt for a while, but she'd get over it, just as she'd get over Ted. Gavin was willing to give her some time.

And then it was finally going to be his turn.

HOUSE FOR SALE BY OWNER.

Stunned, Gavin slowed his truck until he came to a complete stop. Sara had been avoiding him. The friendly talks in the yard had ceased, as had her spontaneous visits to the construction sites. It used to be that Sara couldn't keep away when she saw the crew working on another house on her street. She loved the process of seeing a house built, of everything coming together to make a home, almost as much as he did.

But lately, her pride and embarrassment had caused a wall he was damn tired of beating his head against.

And now she wanted to sell? Like hell.

Cursing to himself, he put the truck in Park and climbed out. He glared at the stormy, cloud-filled skies, then glared even harder at the For Sale sign. Stomping over to her yard, he ripped up the sign and threw it into the back of his truck, then brushed his hands off in a show of satisfaction. Try to sell, would she? Without a single word, without giving him the chance he'd been waiting for? Ha!

He'd been patient too long, that was the problem. He had a plan, and it was time he put it into motion. He wanted Sara, had wanted her for a long time. And starting right now, he was done with waiting.

SARA WAS NAKED, she was wet, and she was frustrated.

She was also alone.

Water sloshed over the sides of the large Jacuzzi tub when she jerked awake. The vivid fantasy she'd conjured in her mind evaporated. She realized it was the loud clapping of thunder that had startled her from the luxury of her bath—and the man she'd been dreaming of.

Disgusted, she shook her head. She'd made a point of avoiding Gavin since that awful, fateful day. She shouldn't be dreaming about him, either. She was tired, that's all, too much overtime at work wearing her down. She'd counted on a leisurely soak in her Jacuzzi tub to ease away her weariness and her aches and pains. But since Gavin had built the house and installed the tub, it was no wonder her thoughts had chased after him again. Now the storm was here, and her fantasy gone, so she supposed her bathtime was over.

Water dripped onto the ceramic tile floor as she threw a worn towel around her body. Sheesh. Even in her imagination, she couldn't indulge a satisfactory romantic interlude. Maybe she should give up on dream men, just as she'd given up on the real thing. Romances, even the imaginary kind, evidently weren't meant for her. Besides, dogs were much more reliable. Unfortunately, like the house, dogs required upkeep. And as much as she wanted one, she wasn't home enough to keep a dog company—or vice versa.

Still dripping, she stomped off to close the windows. Without the cooling breeze, the interior would soon become unbearable, but she couldn't afford air conditioning any more than she could afford a dog.

The evening had turned very dark, and she remembered her front door was open, with only the screen door latched. As she went to close it, she saw the threatening sky, felt a spattering of the rain as it blew in over her porch. She thought again how nice a pet would be, another living thing to keep her company on a dreary night like this. Granted, a dog wouldn't provide quite the same company as a man, but then, a dog required much less maintenance. Dogs weren't as messy as men. They were more loyal and friendly. Dogs never made promises they couldn't keep...

Suddenly she noticed her For Sale sign was

missing. She'd only just put the thing in the yard that day!

Distracted from her daydreams by the possibility of vandalism, she clicked open the lock on the screen door and stuck her head outside, automatically breathing in the churning, moist night air.

"You planning to dance buck-naked in the rain?"

Squealing, she lurched backward and slipped off her wet feet before the familiarity of that deep, masculine voice could penetrate. She would have fallen if her backside hadn't smacked up against the gaping front door.

It took her a moment to regain her dignity— what was left of it—before she cautiously stuck her head outside again. A burst of white light splintered through the night, and she saw her one and only neighbor, Gavin Blake, standing to the side of her door. He was in the shadows, but she would recognize his body, his voice, his *presence,* anywhere. She shivered. *Boy, could she recognize him!*

But Gavin would forever be relegated to the role of her fantasy man. Nothing more was possible. Not after the incident.

She continued to stare, then blinked in surprise as her eyes adjusted. Soaked completely through by the storm, Gavin stood there in a soggy T-shirt and shorts, with a bottle of wine in one large hand.

Good grief! He was too darn gorgeous, too big and imposing and male. He was also the last person she ever wanted to see, other than in her dreams.

But…but there he stood.

Her stomach took a free fall and her heart shot into her throat. She squeezed her eyes shut, but when she opened them again, he was still there, still watching her. ''A pet. I most definitely need a pet.''

Gavin raised his brows, his dark eyes glinting in the shadows, his tone amicable. ''Hey, I hadn't planned on anything so forward, at least not this soon, but petting's good. I'm into petting if that's what you really—''

''No!'' Sara dodged his outstretched hand and ground her teeth together, feeling foolish. ''I meant a pet, as in a dog that might have barked and let me know someone was here.''

His gaze slid from her face to her towel-wrapped body. ''Then I'm glad you don't have a dog.''

With a gasp, she ducked into the house and shielded herself behind the front door. After a long, silent moment, she began to realize he wouldn't just go away, and that she'd once again made herself look ridiculous. She poked her head around the door.

Gavin chuckled. "I'm getting soaked standing here, babe. You going to ask me in or what?"

"Ah… No. Not a good idea." She knew her tone lacked conviction. She'd wanted him, *really* wanted him, for the longest time, but not now, not at this precise moment.

Not dressed only in a towel.

He looked down at his feet, as if considering the situation, then pulled the screen open and stepped inside. "Sara." His tone was chiding. "I've given you plenty of time. I hoped you'd be willing to talk to me now."

She couldn't hold his direct gaze, so she glanced at the bottle of wine in his hand. "What do you want, Gavin?"

"You."

*Oh wow.* Heat washed over her in undulating waves, and she took a hasty, nervous step back, bumping into the wall. She couldn't, wouldn't, look at him. Gavin cupped her cheek with a rough palm and lifted her face. His smile gentle, his voice low, he murmured with a good dose of sincerity, "I like you, Sara. I always have. From the

very first day you looked at this house and proclaimed me a master planner and the best builder
you'd ever come across, I knew we were destined
to be very good...friends.''

*Teasing,* she thought. *Only teasing.* But he *was*
a talented builder, putting that little extra into a
house to make it special. Gavin Blake was, at only
thirty-three years of age, an extremely successful
man.

Sara could still remember the first time she'd
laid eyes on him. He'd shown her around the
house himself because he'd been inside, adding
some touches to the existing kitchen. He'd been
enthusiastic, speaking about his work with the intensity of an artist, while looking every inch the
rugged male in his ragged jeans and work boots.
There had been a healthy sweat dampening his
T-shirt, and he'd smelled *so* good. The cocky way
he walked kept grabbing her attention. He was
confident of his abilities, and with good reason.
What he did was exceptional; he expected the
same of the men who worked for him. He'd
shown her all the perks his housing offered, all
the ways he'd improved on the average plans to
make his creations special.

And she'd fallen instantly in love...with the
house. But she'd also felt a very real attraction

for the man. Gavin had the sensitive hands of an artist, and her fertile mind had imagined those hands everywhere they shouldn't be.

Though she'd been engaged then, and he'd had a relationship of his own, it hadn't taken her long to realize she was planning to marry the wrong man.

But once she'd become free of Ted—the cheating slime—it had been too late. Gavin had witnessed the worst of her, and she was too embarrassed to see him again. And too realistic to keep trying for a romantic future that would only elude her.

But now Gavin was here, in the flesh.

"You used to come and talk to me while I worked." He leaned closer, his gaze drifting over her face. "I've missed you, Sara."

His suggestive tone shook her. She shifted from one bare foot to the other, her naked knees pressed together as she remembered their easy camaraderie, the swell of excitement she always felt whenever he was near.

Gavin watched her, his gaze straying over her shoulders and across the tops of her breasts. She knew her blush had spread, and that it was visible even in the dim light. Then his hand lifted from her cheek and he slid a rough fingertip over her lips. Her breath caught somewhere in the bottom of her lungs, making her dizzy.

"You never used to blush so much."

She thought she should move, but she didn't. She swallowed, then stated the obvious. "I never had good reason before."

"Ah." He turned to look outside, his hands propped on his lean hips, the wine bottle still held securely. "I assume we're talking about the... incident?"

Sara swallowed. It had been a fiasco and the most humiliating moment of her life. It wouldn't have been quite so horrendous, catching Ted with Karen, if she'd handled the situation with a modicum of grace, a little poise. But no. She'd had to go and do her impression of a berserk gardener, grabbing the closest weapon, which happened to be a plastic rake, and chasing a near-naked woman up the middle of the street!

Catching her bottom lip in her teeth, she groaned. The memory was not a humorous one for her, and now here she was, cowering behind a door, making a total fool of herself once again. She would have straightened her shoulders if it wouldn't have caused her towel to slip. "Just why are you here, Gavin?"

He stared at her, or more precisely her mouth,

watching as her teeth worried her bottom lip. He was so tall—over six feet, making her five foot five seem very diminutive. And his wet T-shirt had turned transparent, clinging to his wide shoulders, taunting her with what it both hid and revealed. She could see the dark hair on his chest, appearing so very soft in stark contrast to his hard body.

She knew she didn't want to see what the rain had done to his cutoffs. She felt flustered enough as it was.

His tone was gentle, insistent. "It's been six weeks, Sara. I figured that was plenty of time for you to get over whatever ails you and get friendly again. You've been snubbing me ever since that day."

Her brow puckered at the misunderstanding. "I wasn't snubbing you. I...I wasn't at all sure, after the damage I did, if you'd want to talk to me again." That was a partial truth, because she'd sent him a note of apology and asked for the amount of the damages. She'd found the note stuck inside her screen door, with the message, Paid In Full, scrawled across it. It was sheer embarrassment that kept her away now.

He sighed, then shook his head. "Why don't

we sit down and talk? I'm going to set you straight on a few things.''

Without waiting for her agreement, he kicked off his wet tennis shoes and headed for her kitchen, giving her the perfect opportunity to make a fast break for the bedroom. She did, back-stepping the whole way just in case he turned. And with every foot that separated them, she pondered the possibilities of why he was here. A tiny flare of excitement stirred, but she ruthlessly snuffed it out. Gavin wasn't for her, and he never would be.

# 2

When Sara entered the kitchen a few minutes later, wearing a loose sundress that fell to her knees, she found Gavin leaning against the counter. He gave her a slow, thorough once-over, his gaze intent, his mouth tipped in a slight smile. Then he plucked at his wet T-shirt, pulling it away from his body. His voice was pitched low and deep when he spoke. ''The storm took me by surprise. Do you mind if I take this off so I can get comfortable, too?''

Her mouth went dry. She tamped down the natural inclination to lick her lips, and shook her head instead. Heaven only knew what she might do if presented with such temptation. ''I'm not sure if that's a good idea. There's not much for us to talk about.''

''Of course there is.'' He peeled off the shirt with no thought for modesty or her overly rapt attention. She stared, anxious to catch every riveting detail of exposed male flesh.

She laced her fingers tightly together and held herself still as he shook out his shirt and laid it over the back of a chair to dry. Facing her, he adopted a no-nonsense expression, a stern warning that she was to pay close attention.

The man was half-naked—he had her attention.

"I didn't care about the lamp, Sara. Or the picture." There was a pause, then he added, "I didn't even care about—"

Wincing, she cut him short. "I didn't realize I'd broken more than the lamp and the picture."

"You didn't." He sprawled into the chair, stretching out his long bare legs. He was muscled everywhere, the physical labors of his job keeping him in excellent shape.

She remained standing, too nervous to relax. It was a mixed reaction from the electric charge of the storm, sheer exhaustion, and Gavin's presence. The man had always affected her in one way or another, but since the incident, she'd done her best to repress her more emotional feelings.

Now they were swamping back in force.

Gavin cleared his throat, waiting until she met his gaze before continuing. "I was going to say I didn't mind that you'd chased after Karen."

She sucked in a breath, her shoulders going rigid. "Well, I should hope not! She was..."

was..." Sara searched for a more delicate word than those coming to mind. There weren't many. She finally settled on, "Unfaithful."

He smirked, one brow raised. "She was that. But then, unlike you, I wasn't engaged. In fact, if you'll remember correctly, Karen and I had broken up months before. She wasn't here because of me, Sara, she was only here to visit Ted."

Sara made a grimace, knowing what he said was true. She certainly couldn't blame him for Karen's presence, not that she would have anyway. Blame had nothing to do with her avoidance of him. Humiliation did. "Karen and Ted were the only ones responsible. I know that."

He nodded. "Good. Then there's no reason why we can't remain...friends. Is there?"

Put like that, what choice did he give her? "No. I guess not."

"By the way, whatever happened to lover-boy? I assume you sent him on his way?"

With a sound of disgust, she shook her head. "I didn't have to. When I got back Ted was already more or less dressed and anxious to go. I found him peeking out the door, watching for you I suppose. He crawled out to his car, then slithered inside. He left skid marks in my driveway he was in such a hurry to escape. I think he was afraid you'd come after him.''

"More likely he was afraid of you.'' Gavin slanted her a look, his smile once again in place, though this time it looked more tender than humorous. "You swing a mean rake, lady.''

Another wave of heat inched along the back of her neck, but she refused to look away from his probing gaze.

"Besides,'' he continued, "I wasn't angry at Ted. I'd long since given up my claim on Karen, and in a way, he did me a favor. If he'd hung around, I might have even thanked him.''

Sara stared. "You've got to be kidding me.''

"Nope.'' With no sign of amusement now, he leaned forward in his seat and reached for her hand. "Ted hung himself. He made certain you'd never be able to forgive him, to take him back. I wanted him gone, Sara, because I knew he wasn't right for you. He'd never have been able to make you happy.''

She had to agree with him there. Ted was not the man she wanted to be tied to for life, and in a way, she almost felt grateful, too, because his lack of morals had freed her before it was too late.

Feeling hesitant and uncertain, she asked, "It

didn't bother you—not even a little—that he'd been having an affair with Karen?''

''It made me mad as hell that they hurt you. But for myself? No. Karen is free to do as she pleases, not that she ever felt any restrictions to begin with.''

*He hadn't loved Karen.* Sara was both relieved, and depressed. If tall, beautiful, outgoing Karen hadn't been able to gain his affections, a woman like herself wouldn't stand a chance.

But then, she'd always known that.

She pulled her hand away and tried to fill the silence. ''I applaud your control. I'm afraid I was a little more sensitive about the whole thing.''

''I know.'' He gave her a teasing look. ''I remember.''

Dropping into her own chair, Sara propped her elbows on the table and covered her face with her hands. It all seemed so ridiculous now, but at the time… ''I still can't believe I barged through your house, swinging a rake and raving like a lunatic. It was so unlike me. I've never before indulged in such a fit, no matter what the provocation.''

She heard a low choked sound, and peeked from between her fingers to see Gavin trying to contain his humor. ''What?''

He shrugged, then mumbled around his chuckles, "I was just thinking of the strain you must have been under, keeping all that explosive emotion bottled up."

"I'm not an emotional person."

He sputtered, then lost the fight to keep from laughing. Dropping her hands, she scowled at him, but that only served to make him laugh all the more. At her. She felt renewed humiliation and jerked to her feet, her eyes narrowed on his face. "Go home, Gavin!"

He caught her wrist and tugged her close despite her resistance, trying to rid himself of his smile, and failing. "Ah, Sara. If you could have seen your face that day! It was damn impressive. Outrage and indignation and a good dose of evil intent... Hell, for a second there, you terrified even me. I thought about running for cover along with Karen! But with you shouting accusations and threats so horrid my ears rang, it didn't take me long to realize what had happened, and—"

"And you were amused."

He sobered instantly. "No." Squeezing her fingers, he held her hand close to his side. "I was relieved. You were too good for that jerk and I was glad you realized it before you married him and ruined everything."

Feeling perverse, partly because she didn't understand him, and partly because he was still smiling, she said, "You hardly knew Ted."

"Wrong. I'd spoken with him several times, though not nearly as much as you and I talked. He was a worm. Believe me, Sara, you're better off without him."

She scowled, thinking of Ted's empty promises, and her empty house. Her own gullibility. She'd wanted to be wanted so badly, she'd been willing to be duped by Ted.

Now she merely felt like a fool. "He worked hard to convince me to marry him."

Gavin tilted his head, his eyes intent. "Whatever he told you was probably lies."

She knew that now. Ted hadn't really cared about her at all. Big surprise. "He said we'd make the perfect couple, that love was something that came over time. We were too old to be frivolous, to wait for the kind of relationship you see in movies and read about in books. He said he was as alone and lonely as me, and he convinced me he wanted the same things. A secure home, a lasting relationship. So we approached this wedding business in a logical, no-nonsense fashion. We discussed up-front who would be responsible for various things, and what was expected of each of us. We had the future all mapped out."

Gavin was attentive, staring at her, seemingly fascinated.

She tried to ignore his hold on her wrist, the warmth of his palm and the way his scent made her toes curl. "Ted broke nearly every promise he made. I still wonder why he wanted to marry me in the first place."

"What promises?"

Trying to act indifferent, she shrugged. "You mean apart from the promises to be faithful and act honorably and to stick around through thick and thin?"

Gavin watched her with compassion, and she hated it. She knew she sounded like a woman scorned, but a part of her still felt betrayed, not by Ted, because he didn't really matter, not anymore. But by her own foolish hopes for things that either didn't exist, or else weren't meant for her.

She sucked in a slow, calming breath. "Part of the deal was that I'd buy the house, and he'd furnish it." She lifted her free hand to indicate her almost barren kitchen. A small, aged Formica table and two chairs sat in the middle of the floor. They were ugly and looked totally out of place in the exquisite kitchen Gavin had constructed. The rest of the house was the same, the rooms either near-empty or "furnished" with used, mis-matched pieces.

"As you can see, Ted left before furnishing anything. Even the backyard is barren, and I'd really wanted a porch swing and a pet and a picnic table." She sighed. "I'd thought this could be a real home. Instead it's just an empty shell."

Gavin leaned back, one dark brow raised high. "Let me get this straight. You were willing to hook up for life with a bastard like Ted just for some lawn furniture?"

Sara blinked. Put that way, it did sound rather foolish. Not that he understood it all. She had planned to be a good wife, to do whatever it took to make the marriage work. She'd wanted kids and Christmas, family budgets and a family car. She'd even wanted the struggles that came with maintaining family unity.

She'd gotten nothing but a severe dent to her pride.

She hadn't loved Ted, but she had liked him, and she'd been willing to put every effort into making a solid marriage.

But how could she explain all that to Gavin? He was a man who never wanted for companion-ship, a man who had his pick of women ready to stand by his side. He would never consider accepting a woman he didn't really want, just for something as base as companionship.

"So everything wasn't perfect," she allowed, "I thought we could manage. We would have grown closer with time. We could have made it work." She took a deep breath and mumbled, "I still think the least Ted could have done was furnish a room or two before he ruined everything."

Gavin shook his head. "You can get what you need later, without his help. Be glad you didn't marry him. It would have been a disaster."

He seemed so vehement. But then, that was one of the things that had drawn her to him, his self-assurance and confidence. "You don't understand, Gavin. You've never had any desire to be married."

"Why do you say that?"

Trying to refrain from making another scene, she wiggled her wrist free of his hold and sat down. She wished she'd kept her mouth shut, but now he was waiting for an explanation.

No way did she want Gavin to know just how fascinated she was with him, or the extent of her emotions. She'd suffered such enormous guilt when her feelings toward him had turned...lecherous. She'd never suffered sexual frustration in her life, but when it hit, it *really* hit. Like a tsunami.

It was doubly difficult because her feelings for Gavin had begun as respect and friendship. More than anyone else, more than Ted or any other man she'd known, even more than her parents, Gavin made her feel accepted and liked. She was comfortable around him. She supposed it was only natural that her fertile mind had started to meander into forbidden topics. So she'd felt guilty.

Right up until she came home and found Ted in bed with Gavin's girlfriend. *Ex-girlfriend,* she reminded herself. And then all hell had broken loose. Or, to be more accurate, she'd broken loose, reacting like a demented ogress.

Gavin was watching her, and she had to tell him something. Trying to pick her words carefully, she said, "Karen told me once, when I'd first moved in, that you weren't the marrying kind. She claimed you liked a lot of—" she cleared her throat "—*variety.* She was bragging, because you supposedly cared enough about her to ask her to move in. She said you wanted only the best."

Gavin didn't react the way she expected over the invasion of privacy. He seemed intrigued, and his cocky grin spread wide over his face. "You discussed me with Karen?'' At her noncommittal shrug, he propped his elbows on the table, laced his fingers together, and leaned toward her. ''What else did she say to you?''

''Oh, this and that.'' Actually, thanks to Karen, she knew things about Gavin she shouldn't have known, intimate details that made it more than difficult to be around him, and twice as tough to control her imagination.

At least she didn't have to worry about guilt anymore, since she was now free. And alone. She didn't even miss Ted, which was almost sad since she'd once been engaged to him. But long before she'd caught him with Karen, she'd had doubts about marrying him. He didn't have the same respect for marriage, didn't have the same commitment that she did. To her, marriage meant a lifetime, not until the convenience wore off. Few people seemed able to suffer that small stipulation. Her parents hadn't understood. Neither had Ted.

So along with shedding Ted, she'd rid herself of the idea of marriage. She'd simply given up. Obviously there was something about her that made a long-term commitment impossible. She'd come to the conclusion she needed something shorter term.

Like a blazing, red-hot affair.

She glanced up at Gavin, afraid he might be able to read her mind. But no, he just looked thoughtful. She sighed. Such a gorgeous man, so proud and confident, sometimes arrogant, always fair. But Gavin was more a fantasy man, the perfect male to manifest in a dream, with the reality a million miles away.

Yet…they *were* both single now, and he was sitting right there in her kitchen chair, wearing nothing more than damp jean shorts and a healthy dose of male charisma, insisting they should be friends, which could possibly mean…what? Sara blinked, realizing she'd been quiet too long while contemplating short-term, sizzling, erotic plans.

His wicked grin had turned smug. "So you talked about this and that, meaning…?"

The best defense was a good offense, and she was tired of acting like a ninny. "Gavin, are you actually fishing for compliments?"

"Would you give me any?"

"No." She grinned at his feigned hurt, feeling some of the old camaraderie return. "You certainly don't need me to bolster your ego. You surely know how attractive you are."

He went perfectly still, and his voice turned husky and suggestive. "You really think so?"

She pulled a wry face. "I'm not blind, Gavin. And you don't wear humility worth a darn."

"You never acted the least bit interested. Whenever we talked, it was about the house, or what you intended to do to the yard." He lowered his brows over his dark brown eyes. "Or about your upcoming wedding." He said the last in a disgusted tone, as if the very idea turned his stomach.

"I was engaged! Did you expect me to flirt with you?" Besides, she thought, even after she'd gotten rid of Ted, she knew she wasn't in Gavin's league, not by a long shot. Where he was tall, dark, gorgeous—basically perfect—she was basically plain. Her dark curly hair was always unruly, her eyes a medium shade of blue. There was nothing remarkable about her, other than her slightly crooked front tooth, which certainly didn't fall under the category of sexually appealing traits. She was a very ordinary woman, and he was an extraordinary man.

So why was he here?

Gavin came to his feet, pacing away from her, then back again. He seemed unsettled and she didn't know what to expect. Then he stopped before her.

Crossing his arms over his bare chest and staring down at her, he said, "So we're both available now, right?"

"Uh…"

"And you've already admitted you like me."

Had she actually come right out and said that? She didn't think so. It wasn't likely she'd take another chance on rejection. "I've always liked you, Gavin. You're a nice guy, and you're unbelievably talented…"

"There, you see." He nodded, apparently more than satisfied with her comments.

"But—"

"No buts." He shocked the rest of her thoughts right out of her head when he gripped either side of her chair and leaned down until their noses almost touched. His voice emerged whisper soft, his eyes staring into hers. "I like you, too, Sara. And I want to see you."

Completely frozen, Sara simply stared back. What he said, how he said it, seemed unbelievably seductive. She told herself not to be foolish, not to misunderstand, but she felt her stomach curl up and squeeze tight. For a moment, she thought she might swoon in excitement. Or maybe throw up in sheer nervousness. It was a definite toss-up.

His gaze dropped to her mouth, lingering for a long moment, but to her extreme disappointment, he moved away. "I came today to celebrate. And to convince you to stop hiding from me."

After sucking in two huge gulps of air, she managed to speak without croaking. "Uh, celebrate what?"

"Your freedom. We can start with a toast. I'll pour the wine." He went to the cabinets, and before she could stop him he opened the top drawer, then the next, looking for a corkscrew.

Sara groaned, knowing what he would find, knowing she would be mortified; she resigned herself to the inevitable. She was almost getting used to it.

There was a moment of stunned silence before Gavin turned to face her, a pair of her pale bikini panties dangling from one long finger. He wore an expression of mixed chagrin and incredulous disbelief. "Do you always keep your underwear in the kitchen drawers?"

She would definitely throw up.

There wasn't anyplace adequate for her to hide, though she did consider crawling beneath the table. Of course, he'd still be able to see her, and she'd still have to come out sometime. She didn't think he would just go away.

She dropped her face to the table and covered her head with her arms. "I told you I don't have

much furniture.'' It sounded like an accusation.
''The only drawers in the house are the ones here
in the kitchen.''

Her words were muffled, but she assumed by
Gavin's rough chuckles he'd understood her.
When she heard him opening and closing other
drawers she jumped out of her seat to stop him.
He had a silk camisole in one hand, a garter belt
in the other and a look of profound masculine
interest on his face. The feminine garments
looked very fragile and soft in his big hands. Sara
snatched them away, glaring at him despite her
embarrassment.

He made an obvious, rather measly effort to
hide his reaction. ''Damn, I'm glad I came today.
I'm learning all kinds of things about you.'' He
reached out and stroked the garter belt with a
knuckle, his tone dropping to an intimate level.
''I had no idea you wore such racy lingerie.''

Her face felt so hot, her vision blurred. ''Don't
you dare laugh at me again, you big—''

The sky exploded with a splintered streak of
neon light and the house shook with the accom-
panying thunder. They both jumped, and in the
next instant were left in complete darkness. Sara
held her breath, stunned into silence.

Gavin reached out and felt for her, his fingers

landing first on her throat, then skimming across her collarbone before curling over her shoulder. "Sara?"

"Lightning must have hit a power line." Her voice lowered to a whisper in deference to the fury of the storm.

"Probably."

They stood there in the dark, and Sara could hear him breathing, could feel the heat of his body as he slowly, relentlessly pulled her closer. She could smell his wonderful, delicious, toe-curling scent. Her heart knocked against her ribs and she cleared her throat. "Well. So much for drinking wine. What do we do now?"

It was a loaded question, unintentional of course. But Sara saw the amused flash of Gavin's white teeth. "It just occurred to me," he whispered. "If your underthings are all in here, and you changed in the bedroom, what are you wearing beneath that dress?"

She managed a horrified gasp just before he lowered his head. She knew he was going to kiss her, and she didn't voice a single complaint.

She may have even met him halfway.

# 3

HE WAS RUSHING IT.

Gavin knew he should pull back, give her time to adjust to his intentions, but he couldn't quite get his body to agree with his mind. She was so soft, so sweet against him. And it seemed as if he'd wanted her forever. Hell, it had been forever. A lifetime, in fact.

She was breathing in quick, gasping pants. Touching her mouth with his own, he stifled the small, arousing sounds and gently kissed her. It took all his control to keep the contact light. The feel of her full breasts pressed to his chest tested his resolve.

So many times in the past he'd brushed against her, or shook her hand, or patted her shoulder. Casual touches that left him wanting so much more. He'd teased himself by visiting with her so often, especially whenever she spoke about Ted. Even if the man hadn't turned out to be a jerk, Gavin would have hated him because he had Sara.

He smiled to himself, thinking what a challenge she was, how complex and complicated her personality could be. She'd surprised him more times than he could count.

When she suddenly opened her mouth on his, then grabbed his ears in both hands and kissed him with an intensity he hadn't expected, he wasn't only surprised, he was stunned. And thrilled.

He slid his arms around her narrow waist, marveling at how feminine she was, how perfect she felt to him and with him. Her mouth was hot and damp and clinging to his. When he slipped his tongue just inside her mouth, she groaned. The small sound made him shake. He could have kissed her forever.

But the idea of her underwear continued to plague him, and without even meaning to, he allowed his hands to wander until he cupped her lush backside and discovered for a fact she was naked beneath the dress.

He shuddered again and his body reacted. He pressed her forward against his groin, his hands kneading, rocking her into his hips. His control slipped, but she didn't seem to mind. Things were happening fast, but that suited him. Giving her time, waiting for her to get over her embarrassment, had nearly used up all his patience.

Just remembering all the lonely, frustrated, lust-filled nights he'd suffered through recently filled him with renewed purpose, and he slanted his mouth over hers until she accepted his tongue completely. He explored her with a leisurely thoroughness, fascinated by that small crooked tooth, touching it with his tongue. And then...

She pushed him away. Gavin tried to reorient himself, but the room was dark, and all he could see of Sara was her outline and the gleam of her wide eyes, watching him. He could hear her breathing, as harsh as his own, and knew, even without the benefit of light, she was surely blushing again.

''I want you, Sara.''

She started to step back, but he reached out and caught her. His hand landed first against a plump breast, but he quickly altered his hold to her upper arm. They both breathed hard.

Sara trembled, and even that excited him. He'd never known a woman like her, with her honest reactions and sincere emotions. She couldn't hide her feelings, even when she tried. There wasn't an ounce of guile in her entire being. That alone made her unique.

"Why?"

Her tone dripped with suspicion. Because it was dark and she couldn't see him, he gave in to the urge to grin. He was happy, dammit. After allowing her six long weeks to recover from her embarrassment and any lingering feelings she might have had for her damn philandering fiancé, he was finally with her.

He'd wanted her from the day she'd walked into his house and proclaimed him a genius. It was the first time a woman had noted anything about him other than a physical attribute. He was proud of the houses he built, and so was his family. But no other female had taken the time to realize the extent of his natural talent when it came to his work.

It hadn't merely been the compliment that had done the trick, though. It had been her exuberance, her expressive nature. She was aware of life and the world around her in a way he'd never considered before. She took pleasure in such simple things, in the house he'd built, in her yard work. And he'd watched while she made plans to turn that house into a home with a family...*for another man.*

God, it had eaten him alive, kept him awake at night, and generally filled him with a morbid kind of desperation. She was meant for him, he knew that. And it wasn't just her enthusiasm for him and his work. It was everything she did. Sara was the type of woman children would instinctively trust. Men would gravitate toward her because she was secure and comforting. She drew him with her honesty and her optimism and her generosity…and that lush little body of hers that constantly tempted him to touch. He couldn't discount the body.

He looked at Sara and thought of home and hearth, Christmas and…rumpled sheets on a rainy night. Sara, naked and warm. He groaned. It was an eclectic mix of emotions she stirred, volatile in their power. But knowing he couldn't overwhelm her with his full plans or feelings yet, he said simply, "You're beautiful."

There was no reply, just a telling silence. He sighed, knowing well enough she didn't believe him. "It's true, Sara. Ted probably didn't tell you often enough, bastard that he was, but you're very easy on the eyes."

She cleared her throat, and he waited with a half smile, anxious to see what she would say.

"I'm short."

Ignoring her resistance, he pulled her close for a quick hug, his chuckles rumbling in the quiet of the kitchen. Her head tucked neatly under his chin, his arms looped at the small of her back, he pretended to measure her against him, then nodded. ''You're perfect.''

''Gavin…''

He knotted his hand in her curling hair and tugged until she tilted her face up. Between small, nipping kisses that she greedily accepted, he said, ''You're also very sweet and sexy. It's been hell staying away from you.''

''I had no idea—''

He didn't let her finish, kissing her again until her hands came to his bare chest and smoothed over his skin. Her touch was shy and curious and he knew he'd lose control again if he didn't put some space between them. Damn, now *he* was trembling like a virgin on prom night.

She'd been hurt by Ted, and he didn't want her on the rebound. He didn't want her doing anything she might regret later. And he didn't want her only for an affair.

When he made love to Sara, it had to be because she wanted him as much he wanted her, which was one hell of a lot. Her confidence was a bit low now, and she was obviously gun-shy about getting involved with anyone again. But he could be patient. Being with Sara would be worth the extra effort.

Whispering, because she was still pressed close, her lips nearly touching his, he asked, "Where do you keep the candles and matches?"

"In the cookie jar."

"Ah. Of course. Where else would they be?"

Sara straightened away from him, and he could imagine her fussing with her uncontrollable hair, her nervous hands busy. She moved toward the counter and he heard the *clink* of a glass jar. "I keep them here because the drawers are all full and... Well, I know it doesn't make any sense, but I just couldn't quite bring myself to put my panties in the cookie jar."

"I do understand."

She went still, then asked with a touch of renewed suspicion, "Are you laughing at me again, Gavin?"

He tried to make himself sound appalled. "I've never laughed at you."

"Hah!"

He ignored that. It was obvious he'd have his work cut out for him. "Find a corkscrew, too, and we can take the wine to the other room and get comfortable." He felt her hesitation before she began opening cabinets and rustling through drawers. Very cautiously, she handed him two glasses in the dark, then took his arm to lead the way. It was an unnecessary measure on her part. He knew this house as well as she did, knew exactly where the family room was. And the master bedroom. But he would never refuse her touch, no matter how platonic.

He hadn't been inside much since she'd moved in, though, and he had no concept of the placement of furniture, what little there was. She led him to a couch, then sat beside him.

"I'm sorry I can't offer you a better seat, but the sofa is it." She struck a match, then held it to the candle.

Gavin looked around the room. There was a portable television sitting on a crate, the sofa arranged against the back wall, and one end table next to it with a lamp. The oak moldings along the floor took on a soft sheen in the candlelight. So did Sara.

She turned toward him, her mouth open to speak, and caught him staring. There was a moment of complete stillness, their gazes locked, and then she jerked to her feet, flustered. "I forgot to get anything to put the candle in. I'll be right back."

"Oh, no, you don't." He wrapped his fingers

around her narrow wrist and tugged her back into her seat. "We can use one of the glasses, and share the other."

"But it'd be just as easy—"

"I've already kissed you, Sara, very thoroughly." He kept his tone soft and quiet, his gaze holding hers. "Your tongue was in my mouth. Surely sharing a glass can't bother you that much."

Her eyes were huge, locked with his. "It...it's not that."

"Good." He didn't give her time to form more excuses, and he didn't want her alone in the kitchen, building up her defenses. He opened the wine and filled the glass, then handed it to her. "Here's to your narrow miss at unhappiness, and my escape from monotony."

Quiet and still, she searched his face, her brow drawn in concentration. After a few cautious sips of the wine, she handed the glass back to him. "You really aren't at all upset with me for attacking your house?"

The question overflowed with uncertainty, and Gavin took her hand in his again, rubbing his thumb over her knuckles. "Seeing the look on Karen's face was worth it. You surely did impress upon her the hazards of poaching."

She'd been a stunning sight that day, a virago with a rake, female fury at its finest. He smiled. All he really remembered feeling that day was relief, because he knew Sara would never tolerate infidelity. Ted and Karen, with their lack of morals, had provided him an unhindered chance to attain something he'd wanted very badly.

He honestly couldn't say he regretted the incident, but it prodded him like a sore tooth that Sara had been hurt. The thought of her mooning over another man filled him with territorial and possessive urges that would shock a liberated woman.

Deliberately he took a large swallow of the wine, then handed the glass back to her. She needed to relax just a bit, to take down a few of those walls that kept her so rigid. He wanted Sara to be as he first remembered her—filled with unrestrained excitement and bubbling enthusiasm.

With his arm along the back of the couch, Gavin made himself comfortable, stretching out his legs and making certain his thigh pressed close to Sara's. She was familiar with him as a friend and neighbor. He wanted her familiar with him as a man. *As a lover.*

She didn't move away. When she looked at him again, he dropped his hand to her shoulder in the natural way of offering comfort.

"Quit fretting, honey. You've got plenty of time to find the right man for you, someone who better suits you, someone who'll appreciate you, someone who…"

She shook her head, denying him long before he finished praising her. "No way. I went that route and it was a far cry from matrimonial nirvana. I've given up on the idea of marriage forever. It's nothing but a hoax, anyway. I've decided to stay blessedly single. I'd rather have a pet instead of a troublesome man."

Gavin's heart and breath both froze. He wheezed out, "Excuse me?"

"You know. A little friendly furry pet to keep me company."

"Ah…somehow I don't think it's quite the same."

"Yeah, well. It's a sure bet an animal would be more fun than a husband. More loyal. Steadfast. As long as you're good to an animal, they won't ever leave you."

That was *not* what he wanted to hear. He chewed his upper lip, contemplating her stubborn expression. He hadn't calculated on quite this attitude. For as long as he'd known her, Sara had talked about getting married and settling into domestic bliss. "I can see where you might be a little more reserved now, but it'd be ridiculous to judge every man by Ted.''

''I wouldn't do that! I'm not dumb.'' Then she said in disgust, ''But it's not just Ted. I've never seen one really successful marriage. I'm not sure there is such a thing. But I do know I don't intend to waste my life looking for a husband. Ha! No sir. Not anymore. Pets are less mess, and they're guaranteed to be more trustworthy.'' She punctuated that statement with another long drink, finishing the glass and promptly refilling it. ''It was past time for me to reevaluate and alter my thinking. I did, and I decided marriage is a waste. At least it seems to be for me.''

Now *he* needed the drink.

But Sara had become vehement in her speech, and in-between stating her newly revised plans, which from what he could tell meant avoiding any kind of human commitment, she practically guzzled the wine. Her cheeks were flushed and her eyelids were getting heavy. Bemused, Gavin sat back to watch her.

She made a face with each drink she took, until finally the glass was empty again. She obviously wasn't used to drinking and didn't care for the taste. He didn't want her flat-out drunk, only relaxed. So he snatched up the bottle before she could take it, then pried the empty glass from her hands.

"I understand why you're bitter, Sara, but good marriages do exist."

Flopping back against the couch, she rolled her eyes, then directed her gaze at him. She was sprawled against his side, effectively caught in the curve of his arm. She crossed her legs and swung one small foot. Her words were low and cynical. "Sure they do. Maybe one out of every hundred. And even those aren't really happy, they're just making do. I don't like the odds. Now, a cute little puppy—I could handle that. You make certain they have food and water, clean paper to piddle on, and you can cuddle with them all you want. Done. There's nothing else to it. You love them and they love you. Unconditionally."

It was such a change in attitude for her, he was temporarily thwarted. He wanted to get married, dammit, wanted to settle down for the first time in his life, and now the woman he wanted was dead set against marriage. After all the empty relationships he'd had, he didn't intend to get involved in another. He'd just have to find a way to put Sara back on the straight and narrow.

A good example couldn't hurt. "My parents have been happily married for forty years."

A strange look crossed her face, and her smile wobbled.

"What?" Gavin felt a little uncomfortable with her intense study. She seemed to be contemplating the wonders of the world. "Sara?"

She shook her head, and one lock of curly dark hair fell across her eyes. "Nothing. I just hadn't thought of you that way."

He smoothed the hair back behind her ear, enjoying the intimate contact, the tender touching. It beat the hell out of a handshake any day.

He coasted his fingertips over her fine, soft skin, then continued to cup her cheek. He liked the feel of her, warm and soft and so damn feminine. He liked having her so close and comfortable with him. He could build on that. Friendship was a great start to deeper things. "What way, Sara?"

"You know. With a family."

"Oh?" He touched her ear and the curve of her chin, the sensitive skin beneath it. "You thought I was found under a rock?"

She smiled. "No."

"So how did you think of me?"

She gave his simple question a great deal of consideration before answering. "The eligible bachelor. A playboy, maybe. But definitely not a family guy.'' She frowned, then snuggled against his palm. ''Do you have any brothers or sisters?''

She looked very content, curled up by his side. He wanted to kiss her again, but held himself back. He wanted her to know about his family. He wanted her to *meet* his family. ''No brothers. Three sisters. All older than me.''

She giggled, something he'd never heard her do before. Usually her laughs were deep and throaty and full, not teasing. ''You were the *baby?*''

He tried to look indignant and failed. ''That's right. And it was pure hell fighting for any rights in that house. Do you have any idea how much time three teenage girls can spend in a bathroom?''

''No.'' She looked away, then reached up to cover his hand with her own. ''I was an only child.''

''Hey.'' The way Sara pouted was more enticing than a hot kiss. Damn, he hurt with lust. He looked away from that tempting mouth and stared at her ear instead. It was a cute ear, but it didn't send him into a frenzy of lust. ''I'll gladly give you my siblings. All three of them.'' He forced a laugh. ''Actually they'd love you. So would my mother.''

"I don't know, Gavin. My own mom isn't all that fond of me."

He felt something freeze inside him at the sincerity in her eyes. Lust was forgotten. "That can't be true."

She nodded her head in sharp response. "Yes, it is. She and my dad fought all the time. They were divorced, with joint custody, but they both had busy lives and I...well, I guess I just interfered."

Frowning, Gavin asked, "So you got shuffled between the two of them?"

"Yeah. Dad kept me more than Mom, but even then, it was never for more than a few months. But at least he tried. Once, he even bought me a puppy, to keep me company while he was gone to work, he said. But then a few weeks later, I had to leave because he got a new girlfriend, and Mom had a fit about the dog and...and Dad gave it to a guy who owned a farm. The pup had plenty of room to run around and play, he said."

Oh God. Gavin could feel her pain, could see it in her eyes. He couldn't begin to imagine how a small child, especially one as tenderhearted and sweet as Sara, might have reacted to such a blow. She must have been crushed.

So many things were starting to make sense.

He said very quietly, his eyes on her face, "You really cared about the dog, didn't you?"

She wouldn't look at him. "Of course I did. He was a cute little thing, always running by my side, sleeping in my bed at night. We'd take long walks together, and play together down by the stream. I loved him. But what was really awful was that he loved me, too. He thought I'd always be there for him, but there wasn't anything I could do when Dad took him away. I begged, but Mom only offered to let me get a fish." She peered up at him. "Fish aren't nearly as messy, you know. But they are pretty hard to cuddle."

He'd never guessed Sara might have had a less than perfect upbringing. She was always so filled with optimism. He'd just assumed, with her so determined to marry, that she'd come from a background similar to his. But he realized now her need for a marriage, a home, even a pet, wasn't because she'd seen the wonderful side of that life, but because she hadn't. Ever. She'd been shuffled around and she wanted now to find some stability.

He supposed it made sense, the way she'd reacted to her upbringing. His parents had shown him the better side to marriage, his sisters, too. But still, when they'd all wanted to see him happily settled, he'd rebelled. They wanted him to do one thing, so he fought to do another. It was a response borne more of stubbornness than logic, but being the only son in a family of females had bred that stubbornness. Fighting for your independence in the midst of a gaggle of coddlers was a hard habit to break.

"Is that why you were so anxious to get married? You wanted a home of your own?"

Without his encouragement, she raised her small hand and smoothed it over his chest, tangling her fingers in his body hair. The wine had helped to lower her inhibitions, and she seemed very intent on exploring the different textures of his body. She apparently enjoyed touching him, feeling him. And heaven knew, he wouldn't discourage her from it. But now her gestures had new significance. He wondered how often, if ever, she'd been coddled and held.

Her gaze came up to meet with his, and he caught his breath. Damn, she was so sexy, and she didn't seem at all aware of it.

"I think I wanted to prove to my parents how easy it could have been if they'd only tried. Neither of them spent near the energy on their relationship that they gave to their jobs."

They evidently hadn't spent much energy on

their daughter, either. Gavin leaned down and kissed her forehead, wanting to crush her close, but also wanting her to continue talking. "Sara... I understand how you must have felt. But trying to prove a point to your parents isn't a good reason to marry the wrong person."

"I know. Ted was *nothing* like a pet. Well, maybe a whiskery little rat." Her brow puckered as she considered that, then qualified, "One with mange."

She said it so seriously, and he agreed so completely, Gavin couldn't stop himself from kissing her again. He meant it as a tender touch, a form of teasing comfort, but Sara didn't cooperate. She cupped his face in her hands and licked over his lips, making small, soft sounds deep in her throat that drove him crazy.

He loved her enthusiasm, but he wanted so much more. "Sara..."

"You taste so good, Gavin. I knew you would."

Oh Lord, he'd put himself in a hell of a position.

He knew it was the wine and her own vulnerability making her speak so boldly. Sara was generally rather reserved and circumspect in her behavior. But then, she'd been engaged, and he

knew she would never have betrayed a commitment.

He'd never understood why the house meant so
much to her. Now he did. It symbolized all the
things she hadn't had as a child. And he had built
it for her. His chest puffed up and he felt like
crowing. Surely that had to count for something
in her eyes.

Her soft hands moved across his shoulders, his
chest…his belly. He caught his breath and heard
her laugh. Then he caught her hands. Much more
of that and he'd forget his good intentions.

"You're awfully hairy," she whispered.
"Probably not as hairy as a puppy, though. And
you smell much better than a dog would."

"Thank you."

She smiled at him, their noses only half an inch
apart, and her eyes nearly crossed. He shook his
head, thoroughly exasperated with her, but mostly
with himself. He'd had such grand plans, self-
centered plans, and now he'd have to alter them
a bit to give her the time she needed. He felt the
weight of responsibility, and knew he'd never do
anything to hurt her.

As he came to a few decisions, he watched her
sway in her seat. She seemed to be trying to keep
him in focus. "You're awfully serious, Gavin."

"And you're awfully drunk. You sure as hell can't hold your liquor."

"I know." She didn't sound sorry, only accepting. "Ted used to say I was too prissy. It irritated him that I wouldn't drink with him. But I knew if I did, he'd take advantage of me."

He wished Ted was here now. He wished he'd gone to see him six weeks ago, when he'd first cheated on Sara and hurt her. He hadn't then because he didn't want it to seem as though he'd coerced her final decision in any way. If she left Ted, it had to be because she chose to, not because he made her feel she should.

Pushing her back enough so he could catch his breath, Gavin asked, "Aren't you worried I'll take advantage of you?"

"No. Unfortunately," she said, in a mournful voice, "you're too honorable for that." Then she gave him a slow, exaggerated wink. "But maybe if you drink enough, I could take advantage of you?"

She swayed again as she said it, and nearly fell off the couch. Gavin caught her, then held her upright. "You'd like that, would you?"

"Oh, yes." She pushed his hands away and curled close again, snuggling the side of her face against his chest. "I probably shouldn't tell you this, but I've fantasized about you."

The air squeezed out of his lungs. He gasped and choked before he could manage to say, "Come again?"

Either she didn't notice his shock, or she chose to ignore it. "I think about what it would be like with you." She peeked up at him. "You know. *Intimately.* I was thinking about you just before the storm hit and made me leave my bath. They were *very* nice thoughts, Gavin."

"Ah, Sara..." He sounded like he might strangle on his own tongue.

She sighed. "Karen would tell me all sorts of private things, boasting, you know, and I'd want to smack her because she was living my fantasies."

Damn, he was hard. Really, really hard. It seemed every time he got his libido under control, she'd say something, or do something, or smile— Lord, he loved her smile—and then his body would react. He stayed semierect around her, though she was naive enough not to notice. But Karen had. He wondered if that was why she'd shared intimate details with Sara, to stake a claim of sorts. He shook his head. None of that mattered now, but the small woman curled against him deserved his better judgment, not his lust, which meant he couldn't do a damn thing about the opportunity presenting itself.

He muttered a curse and she heard him. Peering up to see his face, she traced his mouth with her finger and he swallowed hard. She looked so... *ready*. Damn, did she look ready.

And physically she might be. But emotionally, he figured Sara had a long way to go before she would really trust him and accept his feelings for her. Right now, she didn't seem to feel ready for anything more than a house pet. Damn, damn, double damn.

"Sara..."

"Don't you want to know what my fantasies are?"

"No!" She was trying to seduce him, and succeeding admirably. If sex was all he'd wanted, he'd be the luckiest man alive. But he wanted so much more with her. And allowing her to do something she'd regret tomorrow wouldn't aid his case. It'd make him damn happy for one night, there was no question about that, but in the long run, he'd lose out.

He held her at arm's length, trying to convince himself of his own thoughts. "Sara, why don't we talk about something else?"

She pushed against his rigid arms, trying to get closer again. "But—"

Her stomach growled, giving him the excuse to interrupt. "Are you hungry? What time did you eat dinner?" She continued to stare at him a moment, as if the change in topic had thrown her. Then she shrugged.

"I haven't eaten yet. I was too tired when I got home, and I just wanted to soak in the wonderful Jacuzzi tub you installed in my bathroom. But then the storm hit, and I knew I had to close the windows. And then you were here, so…"

Images of her lounging in the spacious, tiled tub—naked and thinking of him—played havoc with his better intentions. A man could only take so much. He cleared his throat and tried to calm his racing heart. "Why were you so tired? A hard day?"

"All my days have been hard lately. I've been working twelve-hour shifts during the week, then volunteering my weekends to the animal adoption center."

Gavin stared at her a moment before dropping his head into his hands. *Wonderful. He'd been pouring wine down an exhausted, hungry woman.* Then part of what she said really hit him. Twelve-hour shifts? He frowned at her, tilting her face up so he could better understand. "You've been putting in a lot of overtime?" She nodded, her eyelids drooping, and he asked, "Why?"

A look of sadness came over her face, and she seemed ready to cry. Gavin vowed then and there never to let her drink again. He'd always turned to mush around weeping women, and with Sara, he felt particularly susceptible.

"I love my house, Gavin."

She said it in a near wail, startling him. "Calm down, babe, and tell me what the problem is."

She threw her arms out, nearly slugging him in the eye. He ducked, then watched her cautiously in case she started to go off the couch again. "I can't afford to stay here. I have to sell my beautiful house."

"What?" He tried to sound surprised because he wasn't ready yet to admit to stealing her sign.

She went on in a rush, making broad gestures with her hands. "I used most of my savings on the down payment. Ted was supposed to buy the furniture, and then pay half on all the monthly bills. The utilities, the groceries, the taxes, the insurance, the…"

"I understand." He rubbed his forehead, frustrated. The house was rather expensive for a single person. His was only slightly larger and he knew how expensive maintenance could be.

He'd come to think of this house as Sara's. Long before she'd actually moved in, he'd made it special for her, added little things, put in extras. He'd known she would love the tiled tub, and she had. He'd thought of her reaction as he installed the beveled glass mirrors. Everything in it, from the time she'd chosen the plans, had been picked specifically for her. The idea of anyone else living in it just didn't feel right. It was almost... sacrilege. "There must be another solution besides selling."

"I've been trying to find one." Sara twisted around in her seat until she faced him. Her sundress had hiked up to her thighs, and one strap hung loose down her pale, smooth shoulder. Her hair, always a little unruly, drooped over one eye. Gavin hid his grin. She looked ready to fall asleep on him, but first, she needed something to eat.

"Come on, Sara." He hauled her to her feet, supporting her when she would have slumped back down again. "Let's go scrounge you up some food."

The candle had formed a small pool of wax in the bottom of the wineglass, and Gavin picked that up to guide them through the darkened house.

The air had gotten hot and muggy; his skin felt damp with sweat. Sara snatched up the wine bottle before they left the room.

He led the way into the kitchen, hearing her hum beside him. "Am I going to find any other surprises in your kitchen cabinets?"

She dropped to a kitchen chair, then shrugged. "Who knows? I can't even remember where I've put everything."

"While I'm hunting up some food, why don't you tell me just how short you are on making ends meet." It was a personal question, but Sara didn't seem to mind. She propped her head up with one fist and regarded him as he searched through the refrigerator.

"It gets a little worse each month. I figure I can make it through the summer, then *pffftt,* I'm out of luck."

Gavin raised one brow. *"Pffftt?"*

"Yeah. I'll be flat broke."

"What about your family? They won't help at all?"

"Hah!"

No. Her family didn't sound like the type to pitch in. And Sara wasn't the type to ask for help. She was an independent little thing. Several times when she'd been doing things to or for the house, he'd had to force her to let him help her. Ted hadn't been anywhere around then, but he seldom was when work needed to be done and Gavin had enjoyed stepping in to fill the slot.

He remembered when he'd gotten his first apartment. His parents and his sisters had all come over with donations, things ranging from furniture to food to cash. And they'd all helped to paint and arrange furniture and prepare the apartment for him to move in. But Sara had no one. He couldn't imagine being so totally...*alone.*

He looked at Sara. Her eyes were closed, and she appeared so serene, so accepting, he wanted to protect her, he wanted to declare himself. But it was too soon. He had to get her used to having him around more, had to give her time to adjust and get over her ridiculous prejudice against marriage.

He found some lunch meat, cheese and pickles and set them on the table for sandwiches. He also poured two large glasses of milk. When he sat in the chair opposite her and began stacking meat and cheese on the bread, her eyes opened. She gave him that killer smile, the tip of her crooked tooth just barely visible. He faltered, then shoved the loaded sandwich at her.

Rather than starting on the food, she continued

to watch him, and Gavin knew he had to divert her attention or he'd never make it through the meal. ''I could give you a loan.''

She bolted upright, nearly throwing herself off the chair. Outrage shone clearly in her expression. ''Absolutely not!''

He'd known that would be her answer, but he wanted to help her. ''Now, Sara—''

''Don't be ridiculous, Gavin. For Pete's sake, we're only acquaintances, despite my rather lurid fantasies. And I have to face facts. If I can't afford this place now, a loan isn't going to help. I'd only end up in the same situation, but then I'd owe you, too.''

He stared, that part about ''lurid fantasies'' still singing through his brain.

''Gavin?''

She was right, but he wouldn't accept her moving. He could alter his plans a bit, but he wouldn't have them completely ruined. He wouldn't give up. He'd spent months mapping out his strategy, and he wouldn't let a little thing like finances get in his way. ''Maybe…''

She held up a hand to stop him. ''It's not your problem. Besides, I've been working on it, and though I'd rather not, I think I may have come up with a solution.''

Thank goodness. Gavin nudged the sandwich toward her again, wanting her to eat. "What are you going to do?"

"I'm going to look for a roommate."

It was a viable solution, he supposed, but... "Do you really want another woman living here?"

"Heck no. Women tend to run a household, to be territorial about where they live. They want to add their own little touches, leave their mark. This is my house, and I don't intend to let someone else take it over. I'd rather go ahead and sell it first."

She gave him a drunken leer, then explained with a flourish, "I was talking about a *man*."

# 4

GAVIN STARED, feeling as if someone had just sucker-punched him in the gut. Was she trying to kill him? Sara with yet another man? *Hell no!* He'd only just gotten rid of Ted-the-despicable. He had no intention of going through that personal hell again.

She gave him a sleepy smile, unaware of how tense he'd become or the agony she caused. He watched as she folded her arms on the table, then rested her head there. She continued to watch him, and she continued to smile. She looked...adoring, and that made him uneasy. After a deep sigh, she said, "I've always thought you were the most beautiful man."

Ridiculously he felt a blush inching up his neck. Thank God it was too dark for her to see, even though her gaze was direct and very intent. "Eat your sandwich, Sara."

She chuckled at his brusque tone. "I'm not all that hungry."

He took a vicious bite of his own ham and cheese. The room was so silent, he could hear himself chew. He also heard her small, dreamy sighs. ''Where, exactly, do you intend to find this *person* who will live with you?'' He couldn't quite bring himself to specify a male.

''I'm not sure yet.'' She gave an elaborate shrug. ''I suppose I'd want someone willing to pitch in, not just expect me to do all the work. And he'd absolutely have to be fun. I can't stand a sourpuss. And he'd have to like pets. I really do want a pet. Maybe a cute little floppy-eared puppy. There's always plenty of them at the shelter that need homes. Too many, in fact. We're nearly full now, and still, every day, someone drops off a litter and…''

''Sara?'' He couldn't bear it if she started crying again.

''Hmm?''

''You're digressing. Where do you intend to find this paragon who'll live with you?''

''I suppose I could ask around at the office on Monday. Or maybe I could run one of those ads.''

''No! No ads.'' Her eyes widened at his tone, and he shook his head, then paced away from the table. ''You don't know what kind of crazy might show up with an open ad.''

He couldn't exactly picture her questioning the men at her office, either. She worked as a secretary for a large corporate firm, and the people there were very stuffy. He knew, because he'd done some contracting for them. How Sara could thrive in that environment, he didn't know. All those suits and exacting regulations would have driven him batty. But for Sara, who always smiled and carried a cheerful disposition, it would be doubly difficult. He supposed it was just one more example of her ability to overcome the obstacles in her life. She'd evidently learned to adapt with her parents, and with her work. But there was only so much adapting a gentle, honest woman like her could do.

And that was why she wanted a dog.

Did she really think having a pet would fill her life? Did she think a dog could act as a buffer against the outside world? He was certainly no psychologist, but it seemed obvious to him Sara wanted to be loved, despite her new resolve not to marry. And since she'd given up on finding a man to fulfill that important task, she was willing to give the duty to a pet.

He snorted. She'd just have to settle for him, and that was that.

But how to convince her? He chewed his lip a

moment, undecided, but he knew in his heart what he would do. He stared at the window and tried to keep his body inattentive to his plans. He cleared his throat. "I suppose there's only one solution."

He waited for Sara to ask him to explain, and when she didn't, he turned to frown at her. "Sara?"

His only response was a soft, snuffling snore.

Amused, he smiled at the picture she made. Her mouth was open, one cheek smooshed up by her arm, and even when he smoothed a hand over her hair, she didn't stir.

Well now. It was Friday. She didn't have to be at work tomorrow, and neither did he. All kinds of possibilities presented themselves, and this time he'd throw nobility out the door. All's fair in love and war, and with Sara, he had a feeling it would be a balancing act of each.

Unfortunately he'd have to start with the war.

THE SUN WAS BRIGHT when Sara opened her eyes. She stretched, then winced at the pain in her head. She felt lethargic and didn't particularly want to get up, which was unusual because she usually woke easily.

She swung her legs over the side of the bed,

noticed she wore a badly rumpled sundress instead of her nightgown and then she remembered.

She'd gotten drunk last night.

*She'd gotten drunk and hit on Gavin.*

Mortified, she pressed a hand to her chest to contain her racing heart, trying to remember everything she'd said to Gavin. Though her head pounded from her overindulgence, it unfortunately didn't obliterate her memory. She recalled several damning tidbits of conversation that had slid silkily off her muddled tongue, and she knew for a fact she'd simply curl and die if she ever had to face him again.

He sauntered through her bedroom door carrying coffee and wearing a wide smile. "Good morning, sweetheart. Did you sleep well?"

She quickly closed her eyes. Death had to be imminent.

Any second now.

If she just waited…

"Sara?"

No such luck. Sara peeked one eye open and saw that Gavin loomed over her, his brow lifted in question. She blinked, caught her breath and her stomach began flip-flopping.

Gavin was still wearing his cutoffs, but now they were unsnapped and only partially zipped.

Partially was enough to make her eyes buggy.

In the full light of morning, he was simply breathtaking. And with a dark beard-shadow covering his lean jaw and his hair sleep-mussed, he looked good enough to be breakfast. He was also waiting for an answer to his question. "I, ah…"

"I slept great," he said. "Your bed is a little short for me, and it was hotter than hell with both of us snuggled in there, but then—" He gave her a wink. "—I could overlook the little discomforts."

Everything in her jerked to a shuddering standstill. Her heart stopped beating, oxygen snagged in her lungs. She was frozen, staring, mouth agape.

He had to be teasing.

Oh God, please let him be teasing.

There was no way he'd slept with her. Surely, even through a drunken haze, she would have remembered such a momentous occasion. She looked directly at him, refusing to flinch, prepared to dispute him and call him on his bluff. She opened her mouth, cleared her throat, and out came something that sounded vaguely like, *"Hmgarph?"*

Gavin set the coffee mugs on the nightstand, then plumped the pillows behind Sara. "Here, lean back and get comfortable. I thought we'd have our coffee in bed.''

*''Hmgarph,''* she said again, because his warm hands had closed around her calves as he swung her legs onto the mattress, settling her despite her stiff resistance.

How many times had she imagined something like this? Something like this...after something much more significant of a sexual nature. She'd dreamed such things, but she'd certainly never considered them actually happening. After all, Gavin was...well, he was Gavin. And she wasn't his type, not at all. She'd even been stretching the boundaries of fiction to imagine it in her dreams.

Yet here he was, and here she was, and all she could do was make nonsensical garbled sounds. If she could only understand why he was here, maybe she wouldn't be so nervous. It couldn't be for the most apparent reasons. Gavin couldn't be interested in her. After all, even Ted had found her so lacking, he'd quickly wandered. Her own parents hadn't deemed her interesting enough to want to have around. There was simply something about her that made people keep their distance. So surely Gavin wouldn't...

He scooted in with her, quite at his ease, his big luscious body taking up a lot of room. He casually handed her a mug of steaming coffee. His smile now was one of satisfaction and contentment. "Now, isn't this better?"

*Better than what,* she wondered, and drank half the cup in one gulp. Despite the heat of the drink, she shivered. It hit her suddenly how cool the room was. Before she could ask, Gavin offered an explanation.

"The electricity came back on about five this morning. It had gotten damn steamy in here, so I turned on your air."

That got her tongue temporarily unglued. "I can't afford to run the air conditioner."

What an inane comment to make, she thought, given the fact she was lying in bed with a mostly naked, utterly devastating man, who surely wasn't there for the usual reasons a man put himself in a woman's bed yet she didn't know why he was really there and couldn't seem to find the wits to ask him.

But her mind simply refused to focus on the real issues. It was too much to take in, and with her heart doing wild leaps around her chest, and her eyes busy exploring every inch of Gavin's hard body, her concentration was nil. Her brain kept screaming, *What happened?* but her heart kept whispering, *I'll bet it was good!*

Gavin took a long sip of his coffee before turning to her. "You can afford to be comfortable, Sara. Remember, you've got a roommate now to split the bills, so there's no need to suffer this heat wave."

*Roommate?* She remembered mentioning the half-baked idea to him, but she never claimed to have found anyone. She wasn't even looking, not since she'd decided she had no choice but to sell. She bit her lip, frowning.

Gavin reached up and rubbed his thumb across the edge of her teeth, freeing her bottom lip and halting her heartbeat in erratic midpump. "I love how you do that." His voice was a rough whisper, deep and compelling. "It makes me hot."

Sara felt like a zombie. A wide-eyed, speechless, sleep-rumpled zombie who could do no more than stare. She swallowed hard to remove the choking disbelief from her throat. "How I do…what?"

"The way you chew on your lip." His big thumb continued to caress her mouth, his eyes watching as she struggled to breathe. "It's so damn sexy. Especially with that little crooked tooth. When I kissed you last night, I felt that tooth with my tongue."

He thought her crooked tooth was sexy? Sara

laughed, comprehension dawning. Of course. It was all a dream! She was probably still in the damn tub, and she'd drown herself before she actually woke up. It would be poetic justice.

"What's funny?" Gavin still looked at her lips when he asked that question, and Sara had to fight not to smile. She didn't want him to think she was deliberately flaunting her sexy tooth.

She laughed again, covering her mouth with a hand. How ridiculous that sounded, even in a dream. She shook her head. "I just realized I must still be asleep, that's all."

Gavin looked up to meet Sara's eyes. *Hot.* His gaze was so hot, Sara hoped she never woke up. She liked having him look at her like that, as if he cared for her, as if maybe he loved her a little. It was a foolish notion, but if dreaming made it seem real, she'd willingly stay asleep.

"When I was younger, the schoolkids used to make fun of my teeth. Mom said she couldn't afford cosmetic dentistry, and Dad kept forgetting. Now that I'm older, it really just doesn't matter anymore."

Gavin's eyes narrowed just the tiniest bit, as if someone had just pinched him, then his gaze dropped to her mouth. "You have a beautiful smile, and the one tooth is only slightly turned, certainly nothing for kids to tease about. I'm glad you didn't fix it.''

She chuckled again, finding his answer as bizarre as everything else that happened. She said, ''A crooked tooth is a crooked tooth.''

Very slowly, Gavin leaned across her and took her coffee cup, setting it on the nightstand with his. As he moved, his broad, hard chest crowded her back and she inhaled his sleep-musky intoxicating scent. She had only a moment to contemplate his motives, and then he kissed her.

Just as he'd said, his tongue pressed between her lips, warm and soft and damp, then probed along the edge of her teeth. *This was no dream.* Sara made that acknowledgment the same instant she decided she didn't care. It was too exciting, the way he teased her with his tongue. She opened her mouth wider, her hands moving against the firm contours of his chest. The hair there was crisp, but soft, tickling her palms and curling between her fingers. And the heat—there was so much heat.

He gave a low groan and urged her closer, then tilted her into the bed until he was lying on top of her.

''Sara,'' he whispered, his lips moving over her cheek, her forehead, her mouth again. He lifted himself onto his elbows, caging her between his muscled arms. With one hand, he smoothed her wildly rambunctious hair away from her forehead, then gave her a tender smile. "You're not drunk anymore."

Sara blinked at the change of subject. Her mind was still back there with that kiss, with the damp heat and his talented tongue and… She shuddered. "No."

"Hungover?"

Since she'd never been hungover before, she wasn't sure. But it sounded vulgar, so despite her pounding head she rejected the idea. "Just tired. And a bit of a headache."

With a slow thrust of his hips, he reminded her of all the places they touched, how intimately they were entwined. "Good. That's good." His gaze lifted to lock with hers. "Now tell me about these fantasies."

Her eyes widened.

With the lightest touch, his mouth brushed over hers. "Last night, you said you fantasized about me. You even offered to tell me what those fantasies were."

Even the air conditioning couldn't counteract the flustered heat she generated, and she hadn't even made it out of bed yet. "I…ah, I was drunk."

His tender smile curled her toes and made her thigh muscles tingle. "I know. But you didn't make it up, did you? Tell me now."

"I should never have said anything."

"I'm glad you did."

"I feel so ridiculous."

"I think you feel very soft and warm and sweet." He pressed against her to emphasize his words, and groaned deeply. "Oh, yeah. Very sweet."

His tone of voice, rumbling and deep, could be lethal. "Gavin…"

"Sara…" He mimicked her, then gave her another light, taunting, tell-me-all kiss. It was almost as if he couldn't stop himself. Sara was considering that possibility, her eyes still wide, when he said, "When do you want me to move in?"

She reeled. True, she was lying flat on her back, and Gavin's weight kept her securely stationed against the bed but still she reeled, at least mentally. Did he intend to keep her off balance all morning? "Uh…what are you talking about?"

His low sigh fanned her warm cheeks, her lips. "I can tell you're not a morning person." His kiss this time lingered, and left her bemused. "That might be a problem, babe, because I definitely am.''

''Am what?'' In truth, she *was* a morning person. But then, she'd never awakened before with a gorgeous man looming around, endearments tripping off his oh-so-suave tongue, while flaunting his too tempting, mostly bare, exquisite body. So she understood her vast confusion even if he didn't. It had very little to do with her sleeping habits. ''Gavin, will you make sense?''

''All right.'' He kissed her once more, short and sweet, then said, ''I'm your new roommate. You do remember asking me to move in last night, don't you?''

When she only continued to stare, waiting for the punch line, he added, ''You were very convincing, shooting down all my arguments, even threatening me with that damn rake once. I had no choice. No choice at all. You insisted I see things your way. And of course, I did. Who could resist a begging woman?''

She narrowed her eyes, knowing she would never beg, not even in a drunken stupor. The rake attack...well, they both knew that was possible. But not begging. ''I haven't begged for anything since...well, since I was kid.''

His expression softened, the teasing gone to be

replaced with tender understanding. "When you begged to keep your puppy?"

She didn't want to talk about that, not now, not when her emotions already felt so raw and exposed. "You're only playing with me, aren't you?"

He gave a sigh of long-suffering affront. "I've been a perfect gentleman, despite your provocation." Then he glanced down at their layered bodies. "Though I'll admit playing with you has entered my mind several times."

*Good,* she thought. Let's play, and you can quit trying to confuse me with things I can't accept. She thought it, but she hoped her silent encouragement wasn't too obvious.

He sat up, then pulled her up, too. She swallowed her disappointment as he moved to her side, trying to concentrate on what he had to say.

"It's all settled. I can get most of my stuff moved in over this weekend, if that's okay with you. Actually I was really relieved when you asked. I was only kidding about you having to beg me. This will work out perfect. It's been a real pain letting people through the house with me living there. I'm not a slob or anything, but I hated having to worry about every little thing I left out of place. And people have no respect for your privacy. They snoop through drawers and cabinets as if they already own the place. This way, with me living here, I'll still be close enough to supervise things, which is why I moved into the model home in the first place, but my privacy will be protected.'' He raised a brow in her direction. ''That is, as long as you don't suffer a penchant for prying.''

Her back stiffened. ''I do not pry.''

''You said you asked Karen personal questions about me.''

''I didn't have to ask,'' she sputtered indignantly. ''She gloated on and on about what a phenomenal stud you are. She practically shoved the information down my throat. I tried not to listen—''

''But she was insistent? How annoying for you.'' His smug grin set her teeth on edge and set her head to pounding. Now that he no longer touched her, she was beginning to see the situation with just a tad more clarity. Still, there was too much she couldn't remember.

''I have no recollection of asking you to move in. In fact, I never once considered such a thing.'' *Not seriously, anyway.*

''Well, why not? We've always gotten along well. Are you telling me you made promises while you were drunk that you've no intention of keeping?''

That was the rub. She wanted to grab this opportunity and take complete advantage of it and him. He was the most compelling man she'd ever met, with a strength and gentleness that formed a potent mix. This could prove to be a page right out of her fantasies. She thought of Gavin's skilled hands, his confidence and capability, and her stomach leaped in encouragement. *Say yes, say yes,* her body screamed.

But she'd made a vow to herself after her breakup with Ted. Never again would she leave herself open and vulnerable to humiliation. A woman should only have to suffer one such incident in her lifetime, and she'd had her quota. She would have to stay in control of any situation, especially those involving men. Right now, with Gavin, she certainly wasn't feeling any sense of real control; she was mired three feet under in deep, dark confusion. He seemed to want her, yet he kept pulling away. Not far away, especially given that he wanted to move in, but just enough to make her want him more, when she already wanted him plenty! It wasn't fair. It wasn't the behavior she was used to from men. Not that she'd been a highly sought after female, but the men she had known had made their intentions plain. Gavin was evidently willing to keep her guessing. But why?

When she remained quiet, Gavin prompted her with a slight nudge to her shoulder. ''Well?''

Feeling trapped, she asked with a degree of obvious caution, ''Did I make very many promises last night?''

His look was suggestive. ''A few.''

Her teeth sank into her bottom lip, and she saw his gaze drop to follow the action, the intensity of that gaze palpable. She immediately hid her teeth behind her lips, but not before their thoughts collided. They were each remembering last night, and the fact he thought she was sexy.

She had to give herself a few minutes to collect her composure, without his disturbing influence, before she made any decisions. Gavin had the power to hurt her much more than Ted ever could have. Ted had been a solution, but Gavin was a desire, a need, a dark craving. To have him, for whatever reason, and then lose him, could be devastating. ''Why don't you meet me in the kitchen after I shower and change and we can…discuss all this.''

''Hell of an idea.'' He was already on his feet,

moving with an air of triumph. "I'll throw together some breakfast."

Her nervousness was enough to choke a cow, and her stomach rebelled at the mere thought of food. "I don't think…"

"Don't worry. I promise to go light." He was halfway out of the room before he added, "I'm an excellent cook, Sara, and I don't mind pitching in. I've even been accused of being fun on occasion, so you shouldn't have any complaints at all."

Gorgeous *and* an excellent cook? But what was all that nonsense about him being fun?

Sara heaved a sigh. She had no idea what was going on. One thing was certain, he had her interest. It was almost too good to be true, though she wanted it to be.

God, how she wanted it to be.

It was terribly risky, especially since she knew deep down that if she accepted Gavin, on whatever silly terms he spoke of, she might end up totally devastated.

Then again, since she was no longer looking for husband material, knowing exactly how futile that endeavor would be, Gavin might very well be the perfect roommate. She couldn't expect a man like him to commit himself to one woman.

Commitment was no longer a requirement. Right? She nodded her head at her own question, but still wasn't convinced. As long as she had her fair share of his time…

Ground rules, that's what they needed. He should be hers exclusively for at least a while. She could glut herself on his masculine charms, then move on to newer game. Men did it all the time.

The thought of newer game actually sickened her. Lately all men had seemed a big turnoff, at least romantically. But not Gavin. Maybe that was because he was such a good friend, too.

She saved the uninteresting, disturbing thoughts of greener pastures for later and concentrated on the glutting part while she prepared for her shower. Now *that* was enough to get a woman wide-eyed and bushy-tailed in the morning. Everyone deserved a little fantasy time, and it looked like this might be hers.

Maybe this would all work out after all.

GAVIN'S PLAN WAS MOVING along rather smoothly. All he needed now were a few ground rules. He had to get Sara to commit, somehow, even if for a short while. He'd work on extending that time as they went along, teaching her to trust him, to trust her own feelings again, and eventually, she would be his. Only his.

It would have to be a unique role reversal, but he planned to hold out on her. She wanted him, that much was obvious. Not as much as he wanted her, which was impossible given his constant state of arousal. But he was more determined, and therefore it stood to reason he could control his reactions better. At least, he hoped he could. He prayed he could. Damn, could he?

It wouldn't be easy. It would be his greatest challenge. More so than building an expansive house, more than doing a renovation, more than...

He grinned, thinking he had likened himself to a superhero, ready to leap tall buildings to rescue his lady-fair—by withholding sex. Actually, leaping a building might be easier than holding out on Sara.

She wasn't a woman who inspired higher levels of celibacy. Not when she went all soft and warm and willing every time he touched her.

But he wouldn't let her use him.

He chuckled out loud, pondering his course of action. He'd force her to be a *gentlewoman* and do the honorable thing, namely marriage. Teasing her would be fun, and a type of stratospheric sensual torture, because teasing her meant teasing himself and he was already on the ragged edge of lust. But with the promise of success, he could take it.

Hopefully Sara couldn't.

He had breakfast ready when she wandered in, looking refreshed and in control. Her cutoffs matched his own, but she wore a pastel T-shirt, where he opted to remain shirtless. He hadn't missed her fascination with his chest, and while he'd always been aware of the attention from other women, it hadn't mattered to him nearly as much as Sara's appreciation. He knew if she hadn't liked him as a man, she wouldn't have given his body more than a single, cursory glance. But she *did* like him, and she did a lot of gawking, not just glancing. So if flaunting his body would help capture Sara, he'd flaunt away without an ounce of remorse.

"Feeling better now?"

She gave him a wary look, then nodded. He was pleased to see she was still uncertain how to deal with him. As long as he kept her off center his odds of success were improved. She didn't want marriage, so he was going to have to sneak it in on her.

"Breakfast smells good."

"Then your appetite has returned. I'm glad. You never did eat your sandwich last night."

When she looked puzzled, he decided to be benevolent and explain. "You fell asleep. I carried you to bed."

Her eyes widened. "Then…?"

"Nothing happened, Sara. Is that what you're wondering about?" He tried for a look of masculine affront. "I told you I behaved myself, though I swear it wasn't easy."

He loved how she blushed. Looking down to avoid his gaze, she pushed her hair behind her ears and fidgeted. Gavin waited, fighting to keep his amusement hidden.

"Last night is…something of a blur. At least parts of it are. Some things I remember clear as a bell, but others…" She hesitated, then forged on. "I have no memory of asking you to move in. None at all."

Guilt swamped him. She looked too confused, vulnerable, too. He considered confessing, maybe giving her some partial truths that would reassure her, when she shook her head.

"It doesn't matter. I'll be glad to have you."

Gavin felt his lips twitch, along with his heart and other numerous, masculine parts of his body. "Have me?"

Her eyes flared, and she stammered, "That is, I mean, I'll be glad to have you *here*."

He raised one brow, his skeptical gaze going to the kitchen tabletop.

"I don't mean *have you*, have you, I mean... You could come here..."

He opened his mouth but she quickly cut him off.

"No! I don't mean..." Slapping a hand to her forehead, she said, "I'd...I'd like you to move in."

He never said a word, giving her the chance to state her intentions outright. She had to make the ultimate decisions of what and who she wanted.

"It will have to be a complete partnership. I'll continue with the house payment myself. The rest of the bills we'll divide down the middle, even the groceries. And we'll have to share all the chores." Then she seemed to consider that. "Although, if you really do know how to cook, maybe we could work out a deal. I wouldn't mind doing the grocery shopping and cleaning up the kitchen if you'd fix the meals. It's the truth, I'm an awful cook."

"No problem. When I can't cook, we'll order in or dine out. What do you say?"

She looked suspicious again, so he tried a very

sincere smile, which only deepened her frown. "That's fine, I guess, but there are a few more things we need to iron out."

She seemed entirely too serious, so Gavin handed her a plate of food, hoping to distract her from her thoughts. "Here, eat while we talk. You need some nutrition after your raucous night of drunken revelry."

She accepted the plate, then breathed deep of the combined scents of scrambled eggs, toasted English muffins and fresh fruit. "It really does smell delicious. I hadn't realized I was so hungry."

Gavin watched her taste everything, then nod approval. He said, "My mom and sisters didn't want to turn me loose when I moved out. It seemed one or the other of them showed up twice a week with homemade meals. I either had to learn to cook for myself, so they wouldn't worry, or be forever indebted to them. I chose to learn to cook."

Sara smiled around a mouthful of warm muffin. "They sound like very nice people."

"Yeah, and I'm spoiled rotten." He waited until she had another mouthful of eggs, then added, "You'll get to meet them next Saturday. They're coming to visit."

She sputtered and choked and coughed while he patted her back. "Are you all right?"

She wheezed a deep breath. "The damn muffin went up my nose."

Gavin bent down to look in her face. "No kidding?"

She took several more gasping breaths, a large drink of juice, then demanded, "What do you mean they're coming to visit?"

With a deliberate shrug of indifference, he said, "Mom always calls on Saturday morning. I knew she'd be worried if she couldn't reach me, so I phoned and gave her this number. One explanation led to another and now she wants to meet you. And whenever my mom interferes, my sisters are close on her heels."

"But…but…I can't meet your family!"

"Why not?"

He watched her search frantically for an answer, and finally come up with, "Because!"

"Because?"

She made an elaborate show of exasperation. "You know why, Gavin. What will they think?"

*That I've finally met the woman I intend to marry.*

He didn't tell her that, of course. If he had, she'd have put a stop to his folks visiting real fast. She was so damn skittish about marriage and family and commitment now. But his family was the better part of him, a real selling tool to a woman like Sara. She wouldn't be able to resist any of them, and they wouldn't be able to resist her. He was certain of that.

Hoping to distract her once more so she wouldn't put up too much fuss, he leaned forward until his mouth was only a hairbreadth away from her lips. ''You've got a whole week to get used to the idea.''

Her eyelids fluttered, then closed as he kissed her. It was a very light kiss, soft and void of sexual intent.

For about three seconds.

Her soft moan shot his good intentions all to hell. When her tongue touched his lips, Gavin stumbled out of his chair and pulled Sara from hers, all without breaking the kiss. With only two steps he had her backed to the counter, trapped there with his body. She was so soft and sweet from her shower, so warm, he couldn't resist touching her.

Tangling his fingers in her dark, curly hair, he tipped her face to the side so his mouth could explore her throat. She hummed a small sound of pleasure, her hands gripping his bare shoulders, urging him closer. He felt the slight sting of her nails.

The distraction worked. In fact, he forgot why he was distracting her.

He kissed her again, wet and hot, his tongue sliding in, imitating what he wanted. What *she* evidently wanted, too, a truth that his carnal side relished. She wasn't drunk this morning, and she knew what she was doing. That thought kept pounding through his brain, driving him.

She groaned and arched into him. It was too much, and he lost control. He was hard, urgent, and he pressed his erection against her soft belly, hearing her groan again and feeling her cuddle him closer. One hand moved to cup her breast, and her nipple was stiff, ready. He started shoving her T-shirt up. He wanted to taste her, to have her nipple in his mouth, sucking, licking…

"Gavin?"

"Hmm?"

Breathless, she whispered, "Are we going to do a lot of…this, when you move in?"

His brain shut down for a single heartbeat. "Aw, hell." Reminded of his plan, he shoved himself away from her, jamming both hands into his hair. Immense frustration rode him, along with total disgust. He'd never get her to marry him if he was so easy. How did that saying go? Something about not buying the cow if the milk was free? Not that he liked comparing himself to a cow. A bull, maybe, but still…

He forced himself to take several deep breaths and face her. She looked aroused. Her lips were a little puffy, her shirt half untucked, her cheeks flushed.

But it was her eyes that grabbed and held his attention. They were bright and clear and filled with hot anticipation.

"Don't do that." His tone was cautious, and he backed up a step. Sara slowly followed. Her gaze remained glued to his, and as he watched, wary, she licked her lips. He felt like a meal set before a starving person.

It wasn't an altogether unpleasant feeling. "Sara…" he warned.

"I wasn't complaining, Gavin, when I asked if—"

"I know." He held up a hand to ward her off, both physically and verbally. If she said much more, if she touched him again, if she licked her lips just one more time, he was a goner. Thankfully she stopped. He wondered how to begin, what exactly to say. He needed her to know how much he wanted her. That was an important fact she had to understand with unwavering certainty. But he also had to make her understand he wouldn't allow her to toy with his affections. There would be no simple fling. If she wanted the beef, she had to buy the bull. Period.

"What is it, Gavin?"

Trying to look stern, he folded his arms behind his back and paced. "You're just coming out of a bad relationship, Sara. People tend to react on the rebound whenever they've been hurt, and—"

"How do you know?" Then her eyes narrowed. "You're talking about your breakup with Karen, aren't you? You said she had stopped being important to you long ago."

Her tone was accusing, and he flinched at his poor choice of wording. "True. Karen didn't mean that much to me. But it was another example of a failed relationship, and I'm getting too old to keep involving myself in dead-end situations. Do you understand?"

She nodded, the movement slow and thoughtful. "But I didn't think you were looking for involvement anyway. And I've already learned all I need to know about these things. If you're afraid I'll get clingy, I promise I won't. I'm not looking for happily ever after. Not anymore."

So. That hadn't just been the drink talking.

Having her reiterate her intentions so plainly pricked his temper. He didn't like the idea that she planned to use him for mere sex. For mere, mind-blowing, torrid, delicious sex. God, he was an idiot. A determined idiot.

Glaring, he said, "That's just it. We're both looking for different things now. And that means we should move slowly."

Her gaze skittered away, and she nodded. "I see."

Exasperated, he said, "No, you don't. I want you, Sara. A lot. That much should be plain."

Lifting her shoulders in a shrug, she said, "I suppose."

"Dammit! You're deliberately provoking me. No, don't try to look innocent." He saw her lips quirk in a small smile, then she frowned again. "Sara." He said her name as a chastisement. "We'll have to get together on this if it's going to work. Do you at least agree to that much?"

"If what will work?"

"Me staying here. We'll need some rules."

"Such as?"

"Such as…" He gestured with his hands, indicating the two of them. "We'll have to work on maintaining some decorum."

"You don't want to kiss me anymore?"

"Oh, yeah," he drawled, letting his gaze linger on her mouth. "I want to kiss you. But it'll have to stop there. We need time to get used to each other. Time to form some sort of understanding, without the past getting in the way."

She raised one brow, waiting for him to elaborate.

"You're going to have to stop making it so easy on me."

"Me? What about you? You're the one who started the kissing."

He smiled to himself, preparing his trap. Give and take, that's what was needed. "Yeah. But you didn't have to go all soft and hungry on me."

"Hungry! I wasn't…"

"Yes, you were. And you made those sexy little sounds." He stepped closer again, one finger touching her warm cheek. "I've kissed other women and not lost my head like that. So it must be you." He had to bite his lip to keep from laughing, she'd gone so rigid, her frown so fierce.

"I'm not going to let you blame me for this, Gavin! Why, you're the one who climbed into bed with me when I was drunk!"

"But I'm not the one who tried to crawl on top of you in the middle of the night."

She sucked in so much air, she choked. "I would never…!"

Nodding, he said, "Yes, you would. *You did.*" Then he added in a low voice before she could get too worked up, "But I didn't mind. Not at all."

"Gavin…"

"Are you going to help me move a few of my things here today?" He threw that in just to change the subject before she could get angry enough to toss him out on his ear. Not that he'd let her toss him out, but accomplishing his goals would be easier if she didn't want to wring his neck.

After blinking several times, she glanced at the clock, then accepted the new topic with a vague show of relief. "I suppose I could help a little. But I have to go to the shelter this afternoon. I'm sorry, but they're counting on me. If I'd known everything that would happen, maybe…"

"No, that's okay. I can manage on my own." And without her help, there was no way he could haul his mattress and box springs down the street. Leaving the sleeping arrangements as they were suited him just fine, at least for the time being.

"If you're sure?"

It was obvious to Gavin she wanted some time

alone, time to sort through all he'd thrown at her over the past twelve hours. "Positive." Then he nudged her plate at her to get her to finish eating. "It seems to me you're a damn picky eater. That won't do. I like to cook and I'll expect you to be properly appreciative of my efforts."

Sara lifted her chin. "I think that's one rule I won't have a problem abiding by."

"Good." He waited until she finished eating, then went to the side of her chair. Time for the next step. He could hardly wait for her reaction. Damn, but he was a genius.

She glanced up at him, her expression alert.

He tried to look serious. "Now, I was thinking, Sara. Maybe you ought to pick out that pet you want today. I know it's kind of soon, but since we'll both be living here, it shouldn't be a big problem or an expense to keep up with one cute little animal. I'll be glad to help out some, to look after it when you're not around, to take it for walks every now and then. What do you think?"

Her eyes widened, and the look of naked excitement that came over her features was worth any amount of nuisance. Gavin didn't look forward to a puppy's accidents, or the chore of housebreaking, but he had thought it an excellent way to start stepping in the right direction. Once she saw how supportive he could be of her pet, she'd realize he wasn't the least bit similar to Ted. And he'd been right.

She leaped from her seat, wrapped her arms around him and gave him a strangling hug. She talked nonstop about whether or not she wanted a large or small pet, male or female. Gavin silently congratulated himself when she rushed out the door, anxious to reach the shelter.

He rubbed his hands together. Things were moving along just as he planned. And as Sara had once told him, he was a master planner.

# 5

SARA GLANCED AT THE HOUSE, but saw no sign of Gavin. She didn't want him to witness her approach. Stealth wasn't her forte, but she felt certain if she could only initiate the idea of this particular animal slowly, everything would go better. No way would she give up her pet now that she had chosen. It had loved her on sight, and the feeling had been mutual. This animal was now hers. But that didn't mean she wanted to fight about it, either.

Her mind whirled with everything the day had brought her way. Throughout her stint at the shelter, her feet had barely touched the ground. She was truly happy. More than that, she was excited. First Gavin, and now her very own pet. And not just any old pet, she thought with satisfaction.

Lugging the heavy box from the back seat, Sara murmured soft soothing phrases to the animal within. Jess and Lou, the couple who owned the shelter, were thrilled when she made her choice. They were also endlessly amused.

That was nothing new, because Jess and his wife had a bizarre sense of humor, a humor that often escaped Sara. But in this instance she hadn't been nearly as obtuse as they'd assumed. And she hadn't minded their good-natured teasing, either, not when they'd supplied all the shots and a thorough checkup on the newly arrived animal for free.

It had been imperative that she take the pet, because if she hadn't, it was a certainty no one else would have.

She'd barely gotten through her front door, huffing with the effort to carry the large box and the weight within, when she heard Gavin approaching. The second she saw his face, she set the box on the floor and stepped in front of it, plastering a bright smile on her lips. "I'm back."

Gavin looked her over from head to toe as if he'd missed the sight of her. "So I see."

His voice was soft, and Sara only blinked when he leaned close and gave her a sweet, welcoming kiss. As he started to pull away, she tilted into him and the kiss intensified.

He seemed determined to keep her at a physical distance.

She was determined to make him relent.

He was in her house. He was available. She figured the least she should do, as an enterprising, healthy woman, was take advantage of the opportunity presented to her.

It was amazing the effect he had on her, she thought, deliberately wrapping herself closer. She hadn't known feelings like these existed until Gavin decided to move in. And since, she'd suffered constant frustration. If he didn't give in soon, she'd go crazy from unrequited lust. Damn his ridiculous ethics.

His hand had just started down her back, encouraged no doubt by her soft moan, when a loud, rumbling growl erupted from the cardboard box.

Gavin froze, his mouth still touching hers, but his eyes wide-open. "What the hell was that?"

Uh-oh. Teatime. She winced just a bit, then whispered, "My pet?"

His eyes flared even more and he took her shoulders, moving her aside and staring down at the box. "What did you get? A mountain lion?"

"Well, actually…" That was as far as Sara got before the box seemed to explode and a massive streak of mangy yellow fur shot out, like a marmalade cannon blast. The huge alley cat surveyed its surroundings in a single derisive glance, swishing its badly bent tail then giving a vicious shake of its monstrous, square head. A small, lopsided pink bow hung precariously over a damaged ear, an ear that was only half there.

Gavin's mouth hung open. "My God."

The cat gave him a look filled with disdain, then strutted past, sniffing the carpet and, for the most part, ignoring the humans.

*"What the hell is that?"*

Sara forced a cheerful expression, hoping to brazen it out, but her words were too quick and nervous to hide her concern. "My pet, of course. Isn't she beautiful? The man who dropped her off today said she was expecting."

"Expecting...what?"

"Kittens!" Sara glanced at the cat, who stared back without a single blink of its large pea-green eyes. Perhaps if Gavin believed the ruse, he'd be more inclined to accept the shabby monster. Surely no compassionate person could turn away an expectant mother. "Her name is Satin."

Gavin sent her a skeptical, slightly horrified look, and Sara rushed on. "She's had a few... mishaps, and being as old as she is, the shelter didn't really hold any great hope of finding her a home. I couldn't leave her there indefinitely, without hope, without prospects. I just couldn't."

The cat chose that moment to give them both its back, walking away with a hunter's stride and sticking its bent tail high into the air. Again, Gavin's mouth fell open, then quickly tightened in chagrin. "Ah, Sara? That cat's about as pregnant as I am."

She already knew that, but she wasn't ready for Gavin to realize it. It was her best excuse for bringing the beast home.

She swiveled her gaze back to him, her brows lowered in stern regard. "If you've gotten yourself into trouble, Gavin, don't look at me. You said our night together was innocent enough."

His smirk proved he wasn't fooled, or diverted. Walking to the cat, he said, "Come here, fella. Let's get that hideous bow off your head."

To Sara's amazement, the aloof cat halted his exit and waited in regal patience while Gavin knelt down and worked the bow free. He ignored Sara as he spoke with the cat. "Satin, is it? More like Satan, I'd say, given the looks of you. You've raised some hell in your days, haven't you, boy?"

The cat's purr was more of a scratchy growl, and the first Sara had heard. It was clear to her the animal hadn't led a pampered life. She'd taken one look at the poor creature and every nurturing instinct she owned had kicked in. The farmer who'd brought the cat in had hoped to escape the shelter's costs by claiming it to be a future mother. He'd dropped off the box and left again all within a matter of moments. But the second the cat had been cautiously lifted free of the cardboard confines, it was obvious he was a tom.

That hadn't deterred Sara. And while she'd pretended to believe the farmer's story, she had put up with her friends' amusement. What the heck? It had gotten the cat some pretty special treatment, and the truth was, she was almost embarrassed to admit she wanted the cat simply because he was alone and unwanted, a feeling she understood all too well.

She felt a strong affinity to a rather homely, bedraggled animal. And that wasn't something she wanted to explain, even to her friends.

Gavin stood again and faced her. "Have you had this animal checked? He looks like he could be carrying any number of diseases."

The cat rolled on the carpet, stretching and luxuriating in his freedom from the bow. Everywhere his big body touched, a patch of dull yellow cat hair remained. He desperately needed a good brushing.

"Jess is a vet, and he checked her...ah him, over. Other than a few scrapes—"

"And missing body parts."

Sara nodded. "Yes. Other than the missing ear, he's healthy. His tail is bent for good and his voice box is damaged, I'm afraid. There's nothing we can do about that. But I have vitamins for him, and a good cat food that should put some shine back in his fur and—"

Sara was cut off as the cat decided he wanted more of Gavin's attention and made a sudden, smooth lunge into his arms. Gavin had no choice but to catch the weight, which was considerable, Sara knew. He staggered, cursed, then reluctantly held the beast. There was a look of distaste on Gavin's face, but still, he scratched the cat's head with his free hand.

Amazed at the cat's show of affection, Sara laughed. "Oh, Gavin, isn't that sweet? He likes you."

"Yeah. Sweet." Gavin grimaced as the cat began to purr again, all but drowning out any attempt at normal conversation.

Satisfaction filled her, and Sara nodded in approval of Gavin's attempt to treat the animal with kindness. "I think he feels indebted because you knew he was a male."

"Uh-huh. Right."

"Don't look at me like I'm screwy. It was obvious he didn't like that pink bow."

"We men feel strongly about that sort of thing."

"Wearing bows?"

"No. Having our masculinity questioned."

"Ah."

"Sara? Did you really believe this beast to be a..."

Before he could finish his question, she had the front door open and headed out. "I have a lot of stuff in the car yet. A litter box, a bed, the food. Will you keep an eye on Satin while I bring everything in?"

"Satin, hell. At least forget that name, will you?"

Chancing a glance at his face, Sara saw Gavin was resigned. She sighed in relief. "What should we call him?"

Looking at the cat as he considered her question, Gavin finally said, "With that vicious purr, Satan suits him well enough."

"He does look like the very devil."

To Sara's surprise, Gavin became defensive of the cat. "Just because he's not some prissy feline shouldn't matter. He's a good mouser, I bet." Then he added, "I had a cat like him when I was a kid. He'd go out every so often and either come home the strutting victor of a romantic rendez-vous, or a bedraggled soldier from battle. Either way, there was always a female involved some-how.'' The cat rubbed his large head against Gavin's chest in agreement, leaving a blotch of fur behind.

''Well,'' Sara said on her way to the car, ''his nights on the town will soon be curtailed. I'm going to have him neutered.''

The cat gave a loud hiss and Sara looked back to see him racing down the hall. Gavin scowled at her, then went after the cat, calling in soft sym-pathy, ''Here, kitty, kitty, kitty…''

Everything was working out, Sara thought. Only two days ago, she was alone, without a sin-gle soul who cared. Now she had Gavin—no mat-ter how temporary that arrangement might be—and she had a wonderful new pet. Not only that, the two males had bonded already.

Now, she thought, feeling lighthearted and happy and half-silly, the only thing missing in her life was lawn furniture, and it no longer seemed so important.

GAVIN LOOKED DOWN at the cat twined around his bare ankles. ''At least you enjoyed my dinner.'' He knew today had to make an impact; it was the first day of their "relationship.'' So he'd made, in his humble opinion, a stupendous dinner, topped by a killer dessert. Sara had eaten a fair portion, had even complimented him on his efforts, but other than that, her attention wasn't where he wanted it to be—on him.

Handing the cat another scrap of meat, Gavin considered his next step. Sara hadn't as yet asked how his moving in had gone. She'd been much too busy settling Satan and enjoying being a pet owner to concern herself with anything as mundane as the new man in her life.

Pushing back from the table, Gavin left his seat and walked to where Sara stood rinsing dishes in the sink. "Are you sure you don't want any help?''

"We had a deal, Gavin. You cooked, so I'll clean.''

"I wouldn't mind helping…''

"You've done enough today.'' She turned, giving him a fat smile. "The meal was fabulous.''

Without giving himself a chance to think about it, he leaned down and skimmed her cheek with his mouth. She smelled so damn good, even after working in an animal shelter all day. He nuzzled her hair, her ear. The catch in her breath was audible, and he leaned closer, caging her between his body and the counter.

Water dripped down his neck when her wet hands settled in his hair, holding him still so she could kiss him. But he darted away. Seeing the disappointment in her eyes, he hid his smile, and his own frustration. But he'd just decided what to do next. "I think I'll go take a shower, then, if you're sure you don't need any help."

"Fine. Go." She returned her hands to the sudsy water, her stiff back showing her disgruntlement.

With a hidden grin, Gavin turned, and nearly tripped over the cat. Satan seemed to want to stay right on his heels, no matter where he went or what he did. He said to the cat, "Sorry, no shower for you. Stay here and visit with your new master."

The cat answered with a grouchy, rusty roar, but he did stay.

Whistling, Gavin went into the bathroom and stripped down. Even with the door closed, he could hear Sara banging the pots and pans around, venting her own frustration no doubt. But that was fine with him. He wanted her so frustrated she wouldn't be able to resist him when he suggested making their relationship more permanent. He wanted her on the edge, willing to overlook her reservations on marriage in order to get her sexual needs fulfilled.

And to that end, he'd do what he had to do.

After quickly showering, he reached for a towel. Leaving the water running, he pulled the door open and yelled, "Hey, Sara?"

There was a moment of silence, then she stuck her head around the hall. She stared at him, her gaze dropping quickly from his face to his wet chest and then down his belly. She stared at the loosely draped towel wrapped low around his hips and mumbled a crackly, "Hmm?"

"I left my shampoo in a box by the front door." His smile was innocence personified. "Would you bring it to me, please?"

He watched her swallow, then drag her eyes back to his face. "Shampoo?" she asked, as if in a fog.

"Yeah. I've got a preference for my own, if you don't mind."

"No. No, I don't mind."

As he watched her hurry away, the cat slipped through the door and wove itself around and between his ankles, leaving his damp legs with clinging yellow fur. Gavin pushed the door wider and tried to nudge the cat out. Satan refused to budge.

"Go on, scat."

The cat hunched back, preparing to leap into Gavin's arms again.

"No!" Gavin backed away, holding the towel with one hand and shooing the cat with the other. He took three steps into the hall, hoping Satan would follow.

"Here you go."

The sound of Sara's breathless voice brought him back around. She held out the bottle of shampoo while staring at his legs. Gavin deliberately widened his stance, letting the towel part just a bit, then saw her eyes flare.

He saluted her with the bottle. "I appreciate it, honey. Thanks."

"Uh…you're welcome."

It was dirty pool to use her attraction for his body against her, but he would do it all the same. He started to stretch, raising one arm over his head and feeling much like a determined exhibitionist. He was just getting into the game, appreciating Sara's attentiveness, when he felt Satan's front paws land solidly against his backside, throwing him off balance. Gavin jerked forward, almost stumbling into Sara, then turned with a yelp when Satan began contracting his claws in his butt.

The problem, the way Gavin figured it, wasn't that the cat had inadvertently scratched him. It was that as he'd turned, Satan hadn't released his hold and as a result the cat's claws were now snagged in the towel, leaving Gavin bare-assed, with only the top corner of the towel preserving his frontal modesty. What was that about best laid plans?

Sara was no help at all; she was too busy ogling.

Gavin thought about abandoning the towel in favor of maintaining his consequence. Being hunched over with your backside exposed while you fought with an alley cat over possession of a towel wasn't a very dignified position, certainly not one to impress the woman of his choice.

A quick peek at Sara showed she wasn't impressed so much as stunned. "Dammit, Sara, get the cat."

She seemed to shake out of her speechless stupor, and then leaned against the wall, folding her arms over her breasts. "Why?"

"So I can get the towel."

She waved a negligent hand, her gaze glued to

his backside. "Just let him have it. That would be easier than untangling you both."

Her words were careless, but when she glanced up, the look in her eyes was pure dare. Now that his options had been severely limited and his plans had gone awry, Gavin knew he had little to lose. Unfortunately he felt embarrassed, which was stupid considering he'd been blatantly flaunting himself anyway. Not that he'd planned to flaunt to the degree of total nudity, but it was too late now.

He couldn't let her have the upper hand, not tonight. He needed to get things moving; the sooner the better. So he stiffened his resolve, gave her a narrow look to warn her of his intentions and released the towel.

To his relief, Sara gave up the game and fled. He'd barely straightened before she rounded the corner of the hall, her wild hair flying out behind her, her startled gasp still filling the air. He frowned down at the cat, who only blinked back. "Any more stunts like that and I'll put the damn bow back on you myself."

The cat quickly followed in Sara's footsteps. Gavin shook his head. "Onward to Plan B. And let's hope it's just a little more successful."

SARA MANAGED TO AVOID any prolonged time with Gavin for the rest of the evening. She took an extended walk with Satan, leading the cat off a thick leash. Then she took her own leisurely bath, soaking for a long time in the Jacuzzi tub until her toes were wrinkled and her muscles finally relaxed.

Still, her mind churned in chaos, playing the same scene over and over again. The picture of Gavin totally nude wasn't something she would ever willingly erase from her mind. The memory of it was enough to send a warmth of anticipation swelling through her body. So it was her own reaction that had her taking long walks and hiding in her tub.

She had literally run! It wasn't to be borne. What had overcome her, she didn't know, but part of it had been self-preservation, she was certain. If she'd stayed, she wouldn't have only looked. Oh, no. Even now, her fingers tingled with the need to touch. The man was too fine for words, too much temptation to resist. She probably would have attacked him. He'd been naked, so therefore unable to offer much defense.

She had no idea what he had hoped to accomplish with his striptease act, but she had no doubt it had been deliberate, though maybe not the part where he actually lost the towel. After all, there was no way he could have prompted Satan to interfere. But the man was up to something. The question was: What?

After she'd finished drying and brushing out her impossible hair, she put on the gown she'd bought herself last Christmas. It was pretty, definitely the prettiest gown she owned, but it wasn't very comfortable. Not that comfort mattered right now. Pretty mattered; comfort ran an insignificant second.

She needed the fortitude of knowing she looked her best before she faced Gavin again. They needed to talk, to clear the air, and she had no wish to wait until morning, giving herself the long night to fret over her cowardly race down the hall. And besides, he might want to kiss her again…or more. She voted for more, not that he'd asked her opinion.

She tried to gather her thoughts and organize them into some semblance of sanity, but they jumped here and there, filled with anticipation and hope and frustration. And as she entered her bedroom from the master bath, her hands busy smoothing the starched fabric of her gown, she stopped in midstride. The sight of Gavin's large, masculine body sprawled across *her* bed in nothing more than leisure shorts with a magazine in his work-worn hands, swept her mind clean of even her insane notions.

He planned to sleep with her again?

She was at first shocked, then immeasurably optimistic. All day, even while picking out her pet, she had nurtured a small hope that Gavin would forget his reticence and let his basic instincts take over. She didn't understand why he kept hesitating. They knew each other well enough, better than many married couples, she thought, considering how much they'd always talked, and six weeks had already passed since her breakup with Ted, assuring she wouldn't react on the rebound, as he'd claimed.

Determined, she sidled toward the bed, waiting for him to acknowledge her presence. The epitome of nonchalance, he held one finger in the air to indicate he needed a moment more to finish the article he was reading.

Irritation was a nasty element to add to an already confused female brain.

''Excuse me.'' When he looked up, one brow raised at her waspish tone, she added, ''What are you doing?''

''Reading.''

He plainly thought she should have figured that

one out on her own. Irritation turned to a tinge of anger. "Okay. Why are you reading in my bed?"

"Oh." He set the magazine down and scooted higher against the headboard. "I wasn't able to move my bed on my own—it's a king-size, you know. All I got transferred today were my clothes and personal items. By the way, I took the closet in the guest room. And since your stuff is in this bathroom, I thought I'd use the one in the hall."

"So...you're sleeping here tonight?"

"Where else?" He crossed his arms and tilted his head, his dark eyes sincere. "Your sofa is much too small. And I'll tell you, the thought of the floor isn't the least bit appealing."

"So why not just sleep in your own house tonight?"

"Because all my clothes and personal items are here. Remember?"

He sounded so reasonable. She wasn't buying it for a minute. He was up to something. Only she didn't know what it was he wanted to achieve, and this time she knew better than to try to outmaneuver him.

Then it hit her. The man was in her bed—exactly where she wanted him to be. She didn't *want* to outmaneuver him.

Trying not to look as anxious as she felt, Sara

pulled back the covers and slid into bed. She felt as stiff as the lace collar on her nightgown, and just as ridiculous. The touch of Gavin's gaze was a tangible thing, and very unsettling.

Without looking, she knew he would be smiling. He would be amused by her nervousness, maybe even a little smug at the effect he had on her. She didn't want to add to his confidence, but she didn't know what to do or how to act. Having anyone close, especially a man, wasn't a feeling she'd experienced much in her lifetime. And this man seemed to genuinely care for her to some degree. The feelings he evoked, those of lust and a craving for tenderness, would be visible in her eyes. She kept her gaze on the sheets, not wanting him to see just how confused she really felt. Then she couldn't help herself and looked at him anyway.

He wasn't smiling; there was nothing of a humorous nature in the way he watched her. Sara started to turn away again, but he captured her chin on the edge of his hand. ''You're beautiful.''

Staring, her chest tight with emotion, Sara bit her bottom lip. His eyes flickered, then narrowed on her mouth. With a harsh groan he turned away. ''Lord, Sara, you make it so damn hard.''

Her eyes widened and her mouth opened.

"Not…" He shook his head, laughing a little, groaning again. His eyes met hers, chagrined and filled with the tenderness she craved. "This is damn difficult. You're making me crazy."

"Gavin…"

"No. Don't you dare say it."

"Say what?"

"I don't know. But it's for certain whatever it is will push me right over the edge. Now give me a kiss good-night and let's get some sleep."

Only her eyes moved, searching his expression, hoping to see some sign that he was jesting. "Just like that? Go to sleep?"

Gavin reached past her to turn off the bedside lamp, then settled his upper body over her, his large hands holding her face. "No," he whispered, his mouth feathering her lips, his breath warm and soft. "The kiss first, then we sleep."

And what a kiss it was. Sara clung to him, feeling the wet touch of his tongue, the rough caress of his fingertips as he tunneled his hands into her hair. It was a kiss meant to prepare her, but not for sleep.

When it ended, she wanted to wail in frustration. But then Gavin pulled her against his side, settling her close and covering them both. His hand smoothed over her arm, and her cheek rested on his chest, the uneven tempo of his heart sounding in her ear.

She hadn't gotten the lust she wanted, but the tenderness was there, enough to wallow in, and for the time being, she decided it was more than enough.

# 6

WAKING WITH A WARM, SOFT body curled close had its advantages. And its disadvantages.

Gavin peered down at Sara's face and felt every masculine instinct he possessed surge to the surface. He wanted her, and his body reacted, painfully so. It was a wonder the sexual pulsing in his lower body didn't rock the entire damn bed. If Sara awoke, there would be no way for him to hide his desire.

But it also felt remarkably right to have her here with him, to breathe her unique scent first thing in the morning, to feel the comfort of her nearness. She slept like the dead. He had hardly slept at all.

The radio alarm buzzed, then loud music kicked on. Turning his head to see the clock, Gavin realized it was almost ten. He needed to rise, to begin a new day of plans. This morning, he intended to overwhelm Sara with his culinary expertise.

A wise person somewhere once claimed the way to a man's heart was through his stomach. Couldn't the same apply to a woman? He would prove to Sara how indispensable he could be, and when she softened toward him, and the attitude of marriage, he'd be ready.

The music hadn't disturbed Sara's sleep. Gavin turned to look at her again, feeling overwhelmed with compassion at her obvious exhaustion. Her cheeks were flushed with the warmth of sleep and there was a darkness around her eyes that showed the level of her fatigue.

She'd been trying so hard to keep it all together, the house, the job, the humiliation from the incident. He wished now he hadn't waited so long to approach her. All he'd done was give her time to chastise herself and build up her defenses. When he thought of her past, he knew she would have a difficult time taking another chance on love.

His thoughts were interrupted by a loud, rasping roar. Gavin looked down at the floor and saw Satan. The cat gave him a blank-eyed stare, then prepared to heave his heavily muscled body into the bed. Since Gavin didn't want Sara awakened yet, he forestalled the cat with a hand and carefully slipped his arm from under her head. She made a slight sound of protest and curled into his pillow.

It was a sunny day and Gavin felt enthusiastic about his chances of making headway. Satan followed him as he pulled on jeans and walked through the door, closing it quietly behind him.

The cat also followed him into the bathroom and wound around his feet, making his morning ablutions more difficult than usual. Satan had the uncanny ability of being right where Gavin wanted to step, each time he wanted to step. Walking had never seemed so difficult before.

He grumbled at the cat, stumbling along down the hall, but the sight that met him in the living room stopped him in his tracks.

There was so much cat fur floating around, the damn cat should have been bald. Gavin looked down, but no, Satan was as shaggy as ever. "Did you have to rub against everything?"

Satan showed his sharp, pointed teeth in what Gavin chose to believe was a feline grin, not a threat. "Okay, so you're telling me you need to be brushed? I'll have to brush the damn house first."

He let Satan out the back door, then checked to see if he had the ingredients for omelets. He'd been known to make a really mean omelet. One bite, and Sara would have to accept her good fortune in having him as a roommate.

Unfortunately, thirty minutes later when he had everything set on the table, the rich aroma of coffee in the air, steam rising from the egg dish, Sara refused to get up.

Gavin shook her shoulder again. "Come on, sleepyhead. I've got breakfast ready for you."

She snared a pillow and pulled it over her head. "Go away."

"Babe, I know you're tired." Gavin did his best not to sound impatient. She'd been in bed for over nine hours, and he knew for a fact she'd slept soundly because he'd laid awake, torturing himself all night by listening to her soft breathing. "I've cooked you breakfast. You don't want it to get cold."

She started to snore.

Gavin lifted the pillow in disbelief. Her eyes were closed, her features relaxed, and her lips slightly parted. A soft, very feminine snore escaped those lips.

Then Gavin saw that her nightgown had slipped down one shoulder and the slope of her breast was exposed. He swallowed hard. Last night, he'd felt that plump breast pressed against his side once Sara had decided to relax. In fact, it hadn't taken her long at all to decide she liked being held close to him, even lying half on top of him.

She'd stayed that way throughout the night, tormenting him, and reveling in the comfort of it. It had been so apparent that she'd never had such comfort before, Gavin hadn't minded staying awake. He'd do it again if she wanted him to. He had intentions of holding her every night from now on.

He gave up on trying to wake her when she rolled onto her stomach in the middle of the bed and sprawled wide enough to cover the whole mattress. He gave one gentle pat to her cute rounded backside and left the room.

This wasn't turning out to be the idyllic morning he'd planned. How could he woo the woman if she wouldn't wake up?

Satan came back in to keep him company while he ate his own omelet. He lingered over the meal, still hoping Sara would awaken. Every so often, he made an especially loud noise, scraping a chair across a floor, banging a plate on the table, but she slept on. Finally, when the eggs were cold, he gave Sara's share to Satan, who sniffed it repeatedly before concluding it might actually be edible. After cleaning the dishes, he located a brush and carried Satan outside.

The cat began purring even before he'd put the brush to his hide.

Another half hour passed before he realized there was no end in sight. Satan looked sleek and well groomed, his large head appearing more square without the benefit of excess fur to soften the effect, and his tail looked more bent for the same reason. But there were still hairs falling loose. His coat was so thick, that no matter how much Gavin brushed, he couldn't remove all the excess. Every time Satan stepped, he shed.

Several old scars were now visible through the smooth coat, however, and Gavin eyed the cat with respect. "You're a regular warrior, aren't you, boy?"

Satan stretched, arching his body high and spreading his considerable claws wide. His mouth opened in a yawn that displayed an impressive array of sharp teeth. All around the yard, hanging from the trees and clinging to the flowers, were clumps of yellow fur, some drifting loose to float in the air like dandelion fluff, rolling across the lawn with the sultry breeze. A small cloud hovered around the porch, the air filled with cat hair as if it were a fine morning mist. Gavin did his own stretching, being careful not to inhale the hair, then turned at a sound from the house.

Sara stood in the doorway, now dressed in loose shorts and a pullover top, a slight smile on her face. "You've been brushing the cat."

Gavin stood and looked down at the cat hairs now clinging to his own body. He had to fan the air so that he could see her clearly. "However did you guess?"

He knew he sounded sarcastic, but he was now a grubby mess, breakfast was over and there she stood, looking so damn desirable he wanted to carry her right back to bed.

The lengths he was forced to go to just to win her over. And she hadn't even had the decency to get out of bed.

"Satan looks very handsome."

"Handsome is not a word that will ever be applied to that monster, but I suppose he looks much better." Gavin studied her closely. She still appeared a little wiped out, as if she'd only just opened her eyes. "You okay?"

She flushed, then quickly nodded. "Yeah, fine. I'm sorry I slept so late. I don't suppose there's anything to eat?"

A sleepless night took its toll on his patience. "I had omelets and muffins and fresh coffee, but you refused to get up."

Sara bit her lip, then looked up at the sunny sky. ''What time is it?''

''Almost noon.''

That startled her. ''Good grief. I'm sorry.''

''It's my day off. I had hoped we could spend some time together.''

''Oh.''

She sounded less than enthusiastic. Then he saw her put her hand to her stomach. ''Are you sick?''

''No, of course not.'' And she flushed again.

''What finally encouraged you to get out of bed?''

''The phone rang. It was…Jess. He wanted to know if I could come out to the shelter.''

''Why? Isn't Sunday *your* day off, too?''

''Usually. But I…well, I already told him I'd stop by.''

Gavin tightened his jaw. The day rapidly dwindled into a dismal failure. ''For how long?''

''I don't know. But I told him I'd be there in about an hour.''

''Dammit, Sara. Why today? Why can't it wait?''

She flinched, then lifted her chin. ''You have no right to curse at me. This is one of the ground rules we should have covered. You don't tell me what to do, and I won't tell you what to do.''

Gavin knew he'd lost his edge, knew he was pushing too hard, but he couldn't seem to stop himself. He'd been sexually deprived too long, dammit, especially considering all the provocation he'd suffered. He was a man on the verge of exploding, and he figured when it happened, his hormones would cover more ground than Satan's hair.

Trying for a moderate tone while his body screamed in frustration wasn't easy. He cleared his throat. Twice. ''I really wish I'd known beforehand.'' *There*. That had sounded calm enough.

She frowned. ''Are you getting a cold? Your voice is all raw and scratchy.''

He stared at her, seeing the concern now in her eyes. If he wasn't so horny, the entire situation might have been humorous. Gavin drew a deep breath, and choked on a cat hair. ''I'm fine,'' he wheezed, when she started forward. Then he waved her off. ''Go on. I've got plenty to occupy me for the day, I guess. Satan shed all over the house. I'll stay here and clean it up. What time will you be home?''

''It's not your job to clean up my cat's mess.''

He stared at her hard. "I'm the one that suggested you get a pet."

"Still..."

It was annoying the way she constantly looked at him as if waiting for him to turn on her. Did she think just because the cat had obliged him to do a little vacuuming, he'd get angry and walk out? After how hard he'd worked to walk in? He snorted.

But then she nibbled on her bottom lip, and he saw that sexy crooked tooth, and forgave her for doubting him. He cursed, then locked his jaw against the unbearable provocation she presented. "I asked you what time you'd be home."

She suddenly exploded. "I'll be home when I'm darn good and ready."

Gavin was stunned by her outburst, but evidently not as stunned as Sara. She gasped, stiffened up like a lightning rod, then turned and ran back into the house. Gavin stood there, wondering what in hell had brought that on.

When he heard her car driving away, he cursed again, this time rather viciously. Satan wrapped around his leg and roared his approval.

Well, hell.

Obviously he wasn't handling things right. He supposed, given his frustration from the night before, Sara might be under the same stress. He'd always thought it rather arrogant of men to assume women didn't suffer the same sexual discomforts as men. Frustration was frustration, whether you were male or female. *And she had wanted him.*

A slow smile spread over his face. Maybe he'd been looking at this all wrong. It was possible making love to her would reach her far better than anything else. It would prove how much he wanted her, and that was certainly important since Sara didn't seem to have a clue about her own desirability.

It would also offer that special closeness that always occurred between two people who really cared about each other. He was convinced Sara did care about him. She was merely being stubbornly cautious.

He'd have to be careful to maintain control, but he could do it. It wouldn't do to let her think their lovemaking was *only* sex. He couldn't let her use him without reaching for the commitment. He wasn't easy. No sir. Gavin Blake was not a man to be trifled with.

And he'd be certain to say all the right words, to treat her tenderly, to show his love.

With that determination, he decided not to wait

for the night. As soon as Sara returned home, he would allow her to seduce him. He rubbed his hands together and grinned in heated anticipation. Satan, being a perceptive cat, grinned with him.

SARA DREADED SEEING GAVIN again. She was never her best at times like these, and having an extra person in the house had only complicated matters. As long as he didn't push her, she could probably maintain control. But if he insisted on cutting up at her, or trying to second-guess her, she might very well explode.

And speaking of exploding...the constant yapping from the back seat had become very wearying. The tiny dog, a mixed miniature breed of some sort, was the noisiest, most rambunctious little creature she had ever seen. And how one little minuscule animal could move so fast on only three legs she didn't know. But boy, this one could.

She was glad Jess had given her the excuse to escape the house, and she was even grateful that they'd given her the chance to look over the tiny dog. But dragging in another animal for Gavin's approval, especially when he'd been annoyed when she left...

The second she pulled into the driveway, she

saw his truck was still there. Everything inside her
started to relax; though she dreaded another con-
frontation with him, she also drew comfort from
knowing she wasn't alone, from knowing Gavin
was inside. But then he stepped onto the porch,
and his disconcerting gaze settled on her face.

Renewed heat rose in her like a tide.

He looked wonderful and strong and handsome;
she looked like hell. Mother Nature had a hand in
that and there was little she could do about her
puffy features and tired eyes. But he didn't know
that. Yet.

And she was certain he could hear the constant,
annoying yapping from the back seat. She tightened her hands on the steering wheel.

Strolling down the sidewalk, Gavin flicked his
glance from her face to the back of the car several
times. Then he stepped around and opened her
door when she didn't show any indication of doing it herself.

For the moment he seemed inclined to ignore
the dog. "You weren't gone very long."

"Nope. Not long at all." Sara tried a smile, but
it felt more like a grimace.

"Long enough to pick up another pet?"

"Well…you see, it's like this. The dog sorta
looked at me, and…well, we bonded." Sara

rushed on, wanting him to understand. "She's had an accident and lost a leg. But she's still plenty scrappy, and she gets around fine. She just needs some TLC. As busy as the shelter is, they can't possibly give her the attention she deserves."

"But you can?"

His tone seemed mild enough, only curious, though he had to raise it to be heard over the racket the dog made. Sara wasn't at all certain of his mood. And she knew her own mood was precarious at best.

She stepped around Gavin and started to lift the cage from the seat. He pulled her aside to do it himself.

She drew a deep breath. "I suppose this is one of those times when you think I should have consulted you first. But you see, there really wasn't any point. I couldn't very well leave the dog there."

Gavin ignored her and started up the walk, holding the cage away from his body and wincing at the continued grating sound. "It's not very big."

"No. She's very fragile."

He said with a touch of sarcasm, "She doesn't sound fragile. Does it ever shut up?"

"Well…no. Not so far." Then she hastened to

say, "But I'm certain once she settles down, she'll get quiet."

Gavin sent her a doubting look as he carried the dog through the house. "You didn't bother to wonder what I would think, but did you stop to wonder how Satan might react to the dog? She wouldn't make much more than a snack for him. He might just mistake the dog for a squirrel or some other rodent. And in case you didn't know, Satan is real fond of catching rodents."

Sara's eyes widened. "No, I hadn't considered that."

"Make certain the front door is closed tight."

Sara started to ask why, then saw that Gavin was about to open the cage, and the little dog was running in circles as if winding itself up for the event. She checked the door, and just as he released the dog, Satan strolled into the room to investigate. The dog shot out as if propelled by force and skittered to a frenzied halt directly in front of Satan.

Then the yapping began again.

Satan endured it with nothing more than a mild look of disgust before he turned away. When the dog made a grab for his tail, Satan turned, punishing the animal with a quick swipe of one paw, then sat back to judge the results.

The dog went instantly mute.

Keeping a wary, worried gaze on Satan, the dog began slinking very slowly over to Sara, its gait awkward due to the missing leg. Satan blinked once in dismissal and curled up in the center of the floor to sleep.

Sara picked up the dog and smiled. "There, you see. They get along fine."

Gavin seemed to be considering her. He watched her for so long, she began to squirm, and finally her temper ignited. "Will you stop it?"

He lifted one brow. "Stop what?"

"Stop trying to dissect me. I brought home a dog. This is still my home, Gavin. I can do as I please."

It sounded like a challenge, a rather nasty one at that, even to her own ears. She was immediately contrite, but it put her on edge having him study her that way.

Gavin dropped his gaze to the floor and his hands went to his hips. She could see his chest rising and falling and knew he struggled to control his own temper. She almost wished the dog would start barking again. It was too damn quiet.

And then Gavin started toward her. She backed up two steps before she caught herself. He took the dog from her arms and set it on the floor. It wandered cautiously, creeping on its three legs, over to where Satan slept.

Gavin tugged her close to his chest. "I don't want to fight with you today, babe."

His voice had been so low, so husky, Sara blinked in confusion. What was he up to now?

He nuzzled her neck and she felt her annoyance melt like a chocolate bar in July. Her heart started galloping. He was such a sexy man, and it was so unfair of him to keep teasing her like this. When his hands settled on her back, then coasted down to her bottom, she sucked in a quick breath and shivered. "Gavin..."

"Shh. You're so tense, honey. Relax, will you?"

Relax? She couldn't possibly relax. Not when he was touching her. At the best of times he could arouse her with only a look, but touching, too? She tried to step away, but Gavin tightened his arms.

"I want you, Sara."

Her mouth fell open, then she leaned back to see his face. "What?"

"I want you. Now."

She continued to stare at him, disbelieving, her anger building to the boiling point, then suddenly detonating. "Of all the rotten, mean, underhanded…'' She shoved him away, seeing his face go blank in surprise. ''Have you looked at me, today? Well, have you? Do I look the least bit attractive?''

Both Gavin's brows shot up. ''Well…yes, you do. You always look nice.''

She leaned forward, jutting out her chin. ''I'm *bloated*,'' she growled in a near demonic tone, as intimidating as Satan ever hoped to be.

''Uh…''

''And at the moment,'' she continued, ''I'm feeling especially mean.''

Just as the dog had reacted to Satan, Gavin backed up, keeping a wary eye on Sara. ''I… ah…''

''I wanted you yesterday, Gavin, but *noooo.* You wouldn't give in.'' She began stalking toward him, and he continued to back up. ''I also wanted you last night. Jeez, I practically begged you. But you couldn't relent then, could you? Oh, no. But now today, oh sure, *now* you want to!''

Gavin stared at her as if she'd lost her mind. ''Sara, what in the world is the matter with you?''

''I can't *today,* you ass.''

Ignoring her insult, he asked carefully, ''What do you mean, you can't?''

Her face felt hot already, but she didn't care.

What a dirty trick. Offering himself when she couldn't accept. Lord, men could be so obtuse. "Think about it, Gavin. It'll come to you."

Her tone had been laced with so much sarcasm, he shouted in return. "Think about what? You're not making any sense. You said you wanted me, well, I want you, too. So what's the problem?"

"I wanted you last night. I'll want you again in a few days. But not until then."

Gavin went still, his frown clearing as understanding dawned, and then slowly, he began to grin. "You're on your period? That's what this is all about?"

Sara punched him in the shoulder. It hurt, like smacking her knuckles against a rock. "Don't you dare laugh at me!"

"Honey—" He reached out for her but she dodged away.

"And don't try to placate me. I'm not in my best of moods at this time of the month."

He bit his lip. "Yeah? I'd already guessed as much."

"Oh, this is so unfair!" she wailed, and the little dog jumped up and chimed in, throwing her head back and howling in a high-pitched, excited whine. Satan decided he'd had enough of all of them, and lifting his massive head, he let loose with a loud, commanding roar.

That was evidently all it took, because Gavin started laughing, and then he couldn't stop. He looked at Sara between his bursts of hilarity, met her outraged gaze, and fell against the wall, holding his sides, roaring every bit as loud as Satan.

Disgusted, Sara stomped from the room. If he was enjoying himself so much, he could just do it without her. She heard him struggling to control himself as she neared her bedroom, and right before she slammed her door shut, he said to the animals, "Now look what we've done. You guys better start thinking of a way to apologize, or we'll all be sleeping outside tonight."

Sara thought that wasn't a bad idea at all.

GAVIN GAVE HER FIFTEEN minutes to calm down. No more, because he was afraid she'd go to sleep again. And no less, because after all, he wasn't a complete fool, despite his recent conduct.

He opened the door without knocking, very cautiously peeked inside and saw Sara curled up on the mattress, holding her middle.

Gavin walked quietly into the room. "I fixed you some warm tea and a sandwich. The tea always helped my sisters."

Very slowly, Sara turned on the mattress to face him. "Needless to say, I feel like a fool again."

"Nope, not this time. It's my turn." After setting the food on the nightstand, he reached out and touched her cheek. "I am sorry, babe. Here I was making grand plans for a day together, and you weren't feeling at all well. I should have realized."

She narrowed her eyes and stared at him. "Grand plans?"

"Never mind. How do you feel now?"

"Men aren't supposed to be understanding about this sort of thing, Gavin."

"Are you kidding? I've got three sisters, and believe me, they forced understanding down my throat until I choked on it. I had no choice at all."

Sara moaned and turned her face away. "This is too embarrassing."

"Don't be ridiculous." Gavin caught her shoulders and hauled her upright, plumping the pillows behind her. "Here, drink your tea." Gavin watched her sip carefully. She still blushed, but of course, she had no way of knowing how he enjoyed taking part in her womanliness.

He regretted like hell that they wouldn't be making love after all. He'd damn near worked himself into a frenzy just thinking about it. Then she'd showed up with that silly dog and he'd almost forgot what he wanted.

But maybe this would work out better.

He wanted to break through all her defenses, and this was a surefire way to get to sleep with her, without becoming sexually intimate. They could talk, and he could hold her, and he could show her how much she meant to him, how special she was.

She watched him over the rim of the teacup, and he smiled. ''The animals seemed to be getting along. They actually started playing a little. That is, if you can call Satan chasing that little squirt playing. The dog didn't seemed frightened, though, even if Satan did sound a bit annoyed.''

Sara picked up the plate with her sandwich on it and broke off a piece of the crust. ''About the dog, Gavin...''

''Does she have a name?''

''I don't know. When Jess and Lou found her, she didn't have a collar.''

''Maybe you should name her, then.''

Sara hesitated, then bit her lip. He could see her mentally girding herself, and he anxiously waited to see what argument she would present.

''Gavin, I know I said a lot about this being my house, and I could do what I want, but I didn't mean to say I wouldn't take your feelings into consideration. I want you to be comfortable here.''

He couldn't help smiling inside. This was the closest she'd come to admitting she wanted him to stick around.

''After I left today, I regretted losing my temper. I sort of thought you might decide it wasn't worth the convenience and be gone when I got home.''

''I'm not going anywhere, babe.''

She looked dubious. ''It's not like me to be so emotional, but—'' She stopped when he started grinning again. ''Despite what you think, Gavin, I am not an emotional woman. At least, not in the normal course of things.''

''I wasn't exactly a prince this morning, myself. I had planned to finesse you with my great cooking ability, but I couldn't get you out of bed. I ended up feeding your very excellent omelet to the damn cat. Then Satan needed brushing, and it turned into a much bigger chore than I'd intended.''

Sara looked very chagrined. ''You fixed me a special breakfast?''

He leaned forward and kissed her. ''Don't

worry about it. Satan showed appropriate appreciation of my efforts.''

''I'm sure it was delicious.'' She peeked up at him, then sighed. ''No man has ever cooked me breakfast before.''

He'd be willing to bet no man had ever played hard to get with her before, either! He merely smiled.

A few minutes later she had finished the sandwich and was once again yawning. Gavin removed the plate from her lap and stretched out beside her. She sent him a horrified look.

''Come here. I'll make you feel better.''

''A man of many talents?'' She looked uncertain, but she did lay down beside him. Gavin moved her around until she was situated against his body, spoon fashion. He laid his large palm over her abdomen and began to gently rub her. Sara groaned.

''Feel good?''

''Mmm.''

She nestled closer and Gavin had to bite back his own groan as her rounded buttocks rubbed against his groin. He kissed her on the side of her neck, then whispered, ''Now that I'm here, you'll be able to rest more.'' It wasn't a very subtle hint, but it was true. She'd realize her good fortune if he had to point it out to her every damn day.

"I don't want to take advantage of you, Gavin."

Her voice edged toward sleep. Gavin kissed her again, hugged her a little tighter. "You can't use someone who's willing, honey. I want to be here, with you."

"And with the pets?"

"Yeah. Even with the damn pets."

Her sigh was soft and dreamy and a bit hopeful, then she said, "I've never known anyone like you, Gavin."

He was counting on that being the case, because he knew, even if she didn't, he had been a goddamn *saint!*

# 7

HE HAD MADE REMARKABLE headway reestablishing their friendship in only a week.

But still, Sara blanched at the idea of meeting his family. They were due to arrive this morning, and while he felt they still had plenty of time, he couldn't go back to sleep.

He'd come to the conclusion, sometime around the middle of the week, that he was most assuredly a man of steel. Only a superhero could have withstood the magnitude of denial he'd forced on his body.

He'd slept, in painful celibacy, with Sara every night.

In some ways it had been unbelievably erotic, holding her, whispering in the dark of the night, discussing the past and the present. He hadn't yet been able to get her to talk about a future. And the more he learned of her childhood, the more he understood.

That was why, even though Mother Nature no

longer conspired against him, he hadn't taken that small step beyond holding her to making love to her. Their relationship became more concrete by the day, but it was still a delicate thing.

Several times Sara had tried taking the initiative, but he always managed to put her off. He wanted to hold out for a declaration of her feelings. He wanted marriage and commitment. He wanted her to buy the cow…er, bull.

But with every day, it got tougher to cling to his high convictions.

And though Sara certainly seemed to like and trust him more now, she was no closer to declaring herself than she had been when he first moved in.

Instead he continually suffered the agonies of unrequited lust, and he honestly didn't know how much more he could take.

Hopefully his family, with all their loyalty and unity and open friendliness would have an impact on her. He glanced at the clock again, and decided he might as well shower and get dressed. But he was loathe to leave the bed, to leave Sara. The effect she had on him was alarming and confusing and so damn sweet. No other woman could stir all his senses the way she did. She left him aching with lust and hurting with tenderness.

He heard a small sigh and glanced back at Sara. He caught her staring.

Trying for a cavalier facade to hide his emotions, he gave her a cocky grin and a wink. "Morning, sweetheart."

Dropping her gaze to his mouth, she reached up and touched one finger to his lips. "Gavin?"

Those slumberous eyes, that gentle touch, were his undoing. Gavin groaned, then accepted her kiss when she leaned up and pressed herself anxiously to him. Her body was sleep-warm and womanly soft. The encouraging sounds she made were low and lazy, still ruled by her slow wakening. When she slipped one bare thigh over his legs he discovered her gown had gotten twisted up high during their sleep.

The week of sleeping together had taken a toll on both of them, so rather than pause to think about what he was doing, Gavin helped to settle her hips over his. Her arms wrapped around his head, her mouth ate at his, kissing him in a way that crumbled rational thought and any resistance. Though what she did was enough to drive any man crazy, there was an awkwardness to her movements that told him she hadn't taken the lead very often. He reveled in that fact.

"Sara, honey…"

''Gavin, please! I don't want to wait anymore.''

She kissed his mouth again, seducing him, holding him still for her assault. She was brazen, voracious, and he loved it.

His hands smoothed down her spine to her backside, lush and firm. Growling, he pushed the tangled gown aside and cupped her, feeling the silkiness of her panties and the warmth of her flesh. His fingers probed.

Sara straightened her arms, her head thrown back, her hips pressed firmly into his. Even with her eyes closed, she appeared stunned, excited and so sexy he no longer thought of long-term plans or goals. She needed him now, and that was enough.

Switching their positions, Gavin pinned her beneath him then began his own seduction. He pulled the tiny buttons open on her gown, baring her breasts. Her nipples were taut and full, and he carefully closed his teeth around one, hearing her harsh groan, feeling the urgency of her hands as she sank her fingers into his hair.

He suckled and tugged, licked and teased. Sara moved beneath him, trying to wriggle out of the gown without breaking contact. She only managed to get it tangled around her belly, but her arms and legs were free. Gavin leaned back to look at her.

Flushed with need from her brows to the tips of her toes, she was a beautiful sight. Her small hands knotted in the sheets on either side of her hips, and her legs were slightly sprawled. He grasped a handful of the gown in each hand. ''Raise your hips.''

Within moments, she was naked, the gown and her panties tossed aside. Gavin wasn't given a chance to enjoy the sight before Sara had grabbed him again, tugging him back to her. He kissed her throat, the sensitive skin below her breasts, her belly. She arched into him, gasping.

Then he felt the cat leap onto the bed. Beside the bed, the dog began yapping, wanting to join the cat, but unable to manage it.

Gavin tried to nudge Satan away with his foot. The beast thought it was a fine game, and swatted at his big toe. The dog howled for attention.

''Scat, dammit.''

Sara moaned softly. ''What?''

It was ironic enough to be funny, but when Satan bit his toe, and the dog began her infernal yapping at top volume, his amusement vanished. Grumbling and cursing, Gavin got to his feet, then met Sara's confused gaze. "Sorry. I need to put the cat and dog out."

"Oh." She scrambled for the covers, but Gavin caught her hands.

"No. Don't move. I swear, I'll be right back." Sara hesitated, then relaxed into the bed, giving Gavin an uncertain smile. After one more long, sweeping look at her body, he hauled the reluctant cat into his arms and left the room, the dog following in his wake.

He refused to think about his decision. Sara was ready, he was sure of it. So what if she hadn't told him she loved him, or even hinted that such a thing was possible? The fact they couldn't resist each other had to count for something. It would be a good bargaining tool for marriage.

The cat kept giving him quizzical looks, and Gavin felt compelled to explain. "Don't take it personal, big guy. You two just happen to have rotten timing, that's all." He sat the cat down and opened the front door. After hooking the dog to her lightweight chain and watching her run out, he turned to the cat. Satan stared back, refusing to budge. Again, Gavin nudged him with his foot. Satan only blinked.

Narrowing his eyes, Gavin murmured, "Now where did Sara put that bow...?" With a disdainful snarl, Satan sauntered out. Chuckling, Gavin was just about to close the door when his mother and father pulled up to the curb. Behind them was another car, and then another.

It looked as though the whole Blake family had arrived. Nieces and nephews began tumbling out the open car doors, and one of his sisters waved. Closing his eyes, Gavin silently went through every curse he knew. It didn't help one iota. Talk about rotten timing.

It took his mother only a moment to reach him, and then he was smothered in a hug. He looked over her shoulder to the end of the sidewalk and saw Satan suffering a similar fate, only it was a group of four children who gathered around the cat. The dog was thrilled with her share of attention, and barked in canine elation. His father and brothers-in-law were slower in leaving their cars.

It was a regular family get-together—not quite what he'd planned, and certainly not how he'd planned it. He cleared his throat when he heard Sara singing along with the radio, then watched as his mother looked in that direction.

"Your new lady friend?"

"Ah, yeah. Mom…we weren't exactly up yet."

"Well, no problem." She patted his shoulder,

her smile impish. "You two can go ahead and get ready while we unload a few things."

Gavin groaned. "Tell me you didn't."

"You know I can't come empty-handed, son. It wouldn't be right. Especially now that you've—"

Sara's voice, slightly outraged, interrupted. "Gavin! Don't you dare change your mind again. You started this, now come back here and finish it!"

Horrified, Gavin stared into his mother's wide eyes, then winced as Sara's voice rang down the hallway again. "You don't want to be accused of being a tease, now do you?"

His mother raised one brow, indicating where her son had gotten the habit, and Gavin could only be thankful the rest of the family hadn't heard. They were taking their time reaching the porch, stopping every so often to admire one of the newer houses being built on the street.

Gavin floundered. "She's, ah…"

"Impatient?" his mother supplied, deadpan.

He shook his head, then walked to the hallway. "Sara!" He had to shout to be heard over the radio. "My mother is here."

The radio snapped off, and after a moment of heavy stunned silence he heard the telltale sounds of Sara rushing around the room. She flew into the hall, wearing only a sheet.

"Sara!"

Running toward him, she yelled, "Don't let her in until I get a pair of panties out of the…" She came face-to-face with Gavin's mother. "Kitchen."

The rest of the family chose that propitious moment to step through the door. Gavin didn't know what to do, and his family, more silent than he'd ever heard the lot of them be, didn't help by simply staring.

Sara turned and let her head hit the wall with a dull thud.

Then his mother asked in a subdued tone, "She keeps her underclothes in the kitchen?"

SARA WANTED TO DIE. She thought, *If this were the Land of Oz, I could just sink beneath this sheet and melt away.* But it didn't happen. It was all well and good to plan a free-spirited affair with a gorgeous, virile man like Gavin, but it was quite another to have to face his mother—*his mother, for God's sake*—wrapped in nothing more than a sheet, the evidence of the affair plain for anyone to see. Only there wasn't an affair, dammit, not yet, because they'd interrupted. Hopefully his mother didn't know *that*.

She felt more than embarrassed, she felt… guilty, and she wouldn't tolerate it. She was a grown woman, and she could darn well do as she pleased.

She sucked in a deep breath, plastered a serene smile on her face, then turned to face the fascinated masses.

Jeez, there were a lot of them.

A dozen sets of eyes were trained on her. She lifted her chin and said a very proper, "Excuse me," then strolled down the hall to disappear into her bedroom. A minute later, Gavin joined her.

She stood with her back facing the door, staring out a window, but she knew it was him. He didn't say anything, and finally she turned to look at him. He leaned against the closed door, his arms crossed over his chest, a pair of her panties dangling from his right hand.

Without a word, Gavin held them out to her.

Sara closed her eyes. "Why am I always being humiliated around you?"

He didn't answer. Sara supposed that was because there wasn't an answer. When she opened her eyes, Gavin was still watching her, and still holding the panties out. She walked toward him, but when she would have taken them from his hand, he caught her wrist instead and pulled her close.

"I'm sorry."

Struggling against him for a mere instant, then giving up, Sara said, "There's no reason to apologize. It wasn't your fault."

"I started things this morning, when I knew my family was coming. And I'm the one who invited them here in the first place."

"No, I started things." Then she peered up at him, giving him a weak smile. "And we both forgot they were coming."

"True enough." He tugged her closer and bent to kiss her neck. "You make me forget everything."

"I can't face them, Gavin."

"Of course you can." He framed her head with his palms and forced her to meet his gaze. "My family loves me, and that means they'll love you, too. No matter what. You have nothing to be embarrassed about."

Pressing her forehead to his chest, she groaned. She didn't understand him, or his reasoning. Surely his family wouldn't care about her just by association. "What did they think when you got my underwear?"

"I explained. It was no big deal."

"But they're all still laughing, right?"

"Naw. If I know my sisters, they're probably figuring some way to blame me entirely, while working up a good dose of sympathy for you."

"Why would they blame you?"

"Because I'm the baby brother, remember? They've always blamed me for everything."

Sara knew he was only distracting her, but she appreciated his efforts. "Even when you were innocent, I suppose."

"Of course. I got blamed the time Pam's bra ended up in the pool when she had her first boy-girl party. And Gina blamed me for scaring her boyfriend away one Halloween night." He said in an aside, "The guy was a real wimp."

"And what about your other sister?"

"Carol and I are closest in age. She just blames me for stealing all her girlfriends away."

"And did you?"

He shrugged. "I let them steal me away a couple of times." Then he chuckled. "But I never let any of them keep me for long."

"Maybe that's what Carol objected to."

"Yeah. They wouldn't come around her again after that."

''They were embarrassed. I can understand how they felt.''

Gavin kissed her ear this time. ''I'm letting you keep me, remember?'' Then he added in a rush, ''Besides, you're made of sterner stuff than they were. You're an iron woman. Shoot, I still remember the way you swung that rake...''

''Stop it, Gavin.'' But she was grinning. ''All right. I suppose I can face them. But it won't be easy.''

''You don't know my family.''

Five minutes later, Sara discovered Gavin was right. He made the introductions with haste, barely giving Sara time to acknowledge each person.

''My oldest—nay, ancient, sister Pam, and her very brave husband, Gary. The two little rug rats who look alike are their six-year-old twins, Stevie and Stephanie. Then there's Gina, who's very obviously pregnant again, and her stallion of a husband, Sam.'' The other men cheered Sam and his potency in high good humor. Sara laughed with them. ''The curly-headed seven-year-old is their son, Chris. And last is Carol, only two years older than me. She's married to Roy, and they have the little redheaded girl, Laurel, who's four. And standing in the corner, smiling at me like I was still twelve, is my mom, Nora. The guy shaking his head—he does that a lot—is my dad, Hank.''

There was no mention of her earlier entrance, and his sisters appeared to accept her easily enough. They weren't the kind to crowd a person, but they were open and accepting and as ready to grin as Gavin always seemed to be.

The brothers-in-law appeared devoted to their wives, attentive and loving. And the children were a boisterous handful. It was interesting for Sara to see the way they all seemed to work as a family. There was no real dissension, but the jokes and teasing were constant. Gina was especially tended to, her husband barely leaving her side, and Sara realized it was because the woman was pregnant. Sam strutted around her like the typical proud papa-to-be, never letting her out of his sight.

Sara knew it would take her a while to get all the names straight, but she found she was already looking forward to it.

Having Satan and the dog, which the kids lovingly named Tripod, gave her instant popularity with the children. And the animals seemed to wallow in their attention. Sara gave the kids a cat brush, and before long, Satan writhed on the ground in blissful ecstasy while they attempted to groom him. She saw the children chasing Tripod around a tree, but moments later they circled back, and Tripod had changed from the pursued to the pursuer. The kids squealed in playful excitement, and Sara could have sworn there was a smile on the little dog's furry face and a look of sheer rapture in her brown eyes as she flashed past.

"They're wonderful animals. How long have you had them?"

Sara turned to Gavin's mother. Nora was the kind of woman who never aged. Though there were lines on her face, and a few gray hairs mingling in with the dark, she was still attractive and still energetic. She made the perfect counterpoint to her Hank, who seemed an older version of Gavin. Both father and son shared a similar height and strength of build.

"I got them both from the shelter about a week ago. I knew the dog was wild, but I didn't think Satan was still this frisky." They both watched as the cat began chasing the dog and the kids.

"Cats are like men, honey. They never stop being frisky."

Sara chuckled, thinking of Gavin. "Amen to that." Then she caught herself, remembering that it was his mother she spoke to. Heat climbed up her neck. "Ah, I don't…"

"You're still embarrassed, aren't you? Please, don't be. We're all just so happy to see Gavin happy. Not that I ever doubted he would be. He's a hedonist by nature. Always has been. But his idea of happy and ours is very different."

Feeling uncertain, Sara said, "You want him to settle down?"

"Gavin told you? Never mind. Of course he did." Nora looked across the yard to where Gavin stood, tweaking his sister's hair, then dodging away from her playful slaps. "I was nothing short of shocked when he called to say he'd moved in with a woman."

Sara chewed her lip. Nora didn't exactly sound disapproving, but still… "He's lived with women before," Sara pointed out, subtly defending their living arrangements.

"Yes, but he never called to alert me to the situation, or to tell me about the woman he was living with." She turned and smiled at Sara. "This is different. You're different."

*Yeah, right. Gavin isn't sleeping with me.* But no sooner had she formed the thought, she had to shake her head. Sleep, yes. Sex, no. But that might have changed if the Blake family had arrived an hour later. Gavin had definitely been ready to give in. And she was more than ready for the momentous occasion. Past ready. Desperate. On the verge of… Ah, but there was still the coming night, and Sara intended to force the issue, if it proved necessary.

"Great news, Sara." Gavin sauntered up, interrupting her thoughts with a warm kiss to her lips. Her gaze darted to his mother, who stood there wearing an indulgent smile for her only son. "The guys are going to help me move the rest of my stuff down here."

"The rest of your stuff?" She knew what that meant, but she could still hope.

"Yeah. My bed and dresser."

Her hope died. Gavin grinned at her crestfallen look, then gave her another kiss. "We'll be back in a few minutes."

Disappointment changed to chagrin when she caught his mother's amusement. Good grief. Fumbling through her explanations, Sara said, "He, ah…"

Nora waved away Sara's concerns. "I know my son very well, Sara. He's a rascal. Don't let it bother you." Then she added, "What do your parents think of your house?"

"They haven't seen it."

Nora merely blinked. "Oh?" But it was a very maternal inquiry, and Sara found herself drawn in.

"We're not really…close."

"Oh, that's too bad. They live far away?"

"No." There was something about Nora that invited confidence. Her questions were genuine, prompted by concern, not idle curiosity. Sara bit her lip, then blurted, "My parents live close, but they're not really interested in me or what I'm doing."

Nora studied Sara's face for a moment, then she shook her head. "Sometimes parents do the dumbest things. But you know, it's only because we're human. I can't tell you the number of mistakes I made with my children. Why, you could fill the Taj Mahal with my goofs."

Sara did a double take. "Gavin told me he had a wonderful childhood!"

"Oh, I'm sure he did. Still, there were plenty of times when he thought I was picking on him. All the kids have accused me of having a favorite, or treating them unfairly at one time or another. That's all part of being a child, I suppose. Kids view the world through a narrow lens, never noticing all the outlying problems that parents might have to deal with. Their feelings get hurt, and they think we don't care, when actually, we didn't even realize how they were feeling.''

Sara thought of her parents' divorce, and how distracted they both became after that. Then she shook her head. ''I understand what you're saying, Mrs. Blake. But my parents really didn't care.''

''I can't believe that. No, you're a very nice girl, and children seldom get to be that way without some love and guidance.''

The grin tugged at her lips, but Sara held it back. ''What makes you so certain I'm a nice girl?''

''Gavin's with you, isn't he? And even though I have to admit to making mistakes, I know I didn't raise any dummies.'' She softened those words by asking, ''Have you ever told your parents how you feel?''

''Well…no. There would be no point to it.''

''Have you called them and invited them over? Do you try to go see them?''

Again, all Sara could do was shake her head.

''You know, honey, they could be thinking back on the past, seeing things now that they couldn't see then, and wondering if you could possibly still love them.'' Nora patted her cheek. ''I have no idea what problems you had with your parents, but why don't you think about it? And remember that nobody's perfect, parents least of all.''

Sara remembered those words the rest of the day. They kept coming back to her, over and over again. She realized she wanted to believe there might be some chance. She wanted the kind of relationship she'd just witnessed between Gavin and his family. That would be stretching it a bit, but perhaps there would be something, some closeness, to work with if she only initiated it.

She understood now why Gavin was so special, so understanding and accepting and confident. And seeing all that only made her want him more.

GAVIN HELPED BUCKLE his youngest niece into her car seat, then allowed her to give him a wet smacking kiss on his cheek. Carol stood on the sidewalk, saying her final goodbyes to Sara. Being closest in age, the two of them had really hit it off, and Gavin knew Carol would come calling again. All in all, he was pleased with the way Sara had been accepted.

His family had spent most of the afternoon with them, and each of his sisters had taken a turn grilling Sara for information. But Sara hadn't seemed uncomfortable with them. In fact, he'd seen her laughing out loud several times.

Lunch had consisted of takeout chicken, and they'd eaten picnic style on the back lawn. Satan had wandered from person to person, glutting himself on tidbits of food, then amusing everyone with his dexterity as he faced a mock battle with a chunk of chicken. He rolled on the ground, throwing the food in the air and then swatting it around. For a while there, it had seemed the chicken might actually win, but in the end, Satan proved the victor.

Tripod was just the opposite. She found a lap and refused to leave it. She was pampered and petted and hand-fed until Gavin feared she might pop.

When Sara had apologized for not having any lawn furniture, Gavin saw his mother's eyes light up and knew some would be arriving soon. He wondered how Sara would receive the gift, if she'd understand the spirit in which it was given.

The cars began driving away in a loud farewell ceremony of honking horns and cheerful children and waving hands. Carol embraced Sara, who looked somewhat startled by the gesture, but she returned the hug. Then Carol came to the curb with Gavin.

"Don't blow this one, brother."

Gavin grinned. "I don't intend to."

"Ah. So it is like that. Mom said so, but I wasn't sure."

Gavin looked back at Sara. She stood on the sidewalk, watching him and Carol. She was keeping herself apart, he realized. She refused to accept all of him. He hated it.

Smacking Carol's backside, he said, "Go on and get out of here. I have things to do."

"Uh-huh. In that big king-size bed you had Roy help you move?"

"Despite being married and a mother, you're too young to know about such things."

Carol merely snorted, then climbed into the car. She waved to Sara and Gavin as Roy pulled away from the curb.

When Gavin reached Sara's side again, she said, "Your sister is nice."

"Carol? She's a pain in the ass, but I love her." He put his arm around Sara's shoulders and started her toward the house. "So what about the rest of my family? Did they overwhelm you?"

"Of course. But then, you knew they would."

They passed the animals lying beneath a tree. Satan was sprawled on his back, his mouth open, snoring loud enough to scare away every bird in a five-mile radius. Tripod had her head resting on his belly. She watched lazily as the humans walked by, but didn't bother to follow. Gavin chuckled. ''They look pooped.''

''I think they both had more fun today than they're used to.''

''And what about you?'' They had reached the porch, and Gavin urged her up the steps. ''Did you have fun?''

They stopped in the doorway. Sunlight slanted over the porch, diffused through the thick leaves of the tree Satan rested beneath. Gavin still had his arm around her shoulders, and he felt as much as saw her small shrug.

''Sara?'' He felt concern, wondering for the first time if he'd done the right thing by bringing his family around so soon. It had seemed a perfect gambit, a way to prove to Sara that happy marriages did exist, that families could and should be a wonderful thing. But now, he wasn't so sure.

Sara took a small step toward him and he automatically put his arms around her, giving her comfort if that was what she needed. Maybe his plans had backfired. Maybe his family had only reminded her of what she didn't have, of how little her parents supposedly cared.

Hugging her tighter, feeling her body pressed

to his from knees to chest, he stroked her hair.
"What's wrong, honey? Did someone say or do
something to upset you?"

She nodded, and Gavin felt his stomach tighten.
"Tell me what happened." If one of his sisters
had said something stupid to upset her, he'd…

"It was the men."

"My brothers-in-law?" Now that surprised
him. They were all such laid-back, easygoing
guys. He couldn't imagine them treating Sara with
anything less than friendly respect. It had to be a
misunderstanding. He cupped her chin, then
tipped her head back so he could see her face.
She wore the most wicked smile he'd ever seen
on a woman.

"Your family is wonderful, Gavin. But I didn't
appreciate the men fetching your bed. I hope you
weren't actually planning on using it, because I'll
have to say right now, up-front, I won't stand for
it."

God, she was good. How any woman could
look so innocent while she blatantly seduced a
man was beyond him. Her cheeks were pink, but
her eyes were direct, proving she didn't intend to
back down.

That suited Gavin just fine.

"I wanted you to have a choice, babe." He

searched her face, trying to read her expressions. He needed her to understand, to know how important this was to him. Sara wasn't just another convenient woman, she was *his* woman. Forever. ''I didn't want you to make love with me just because circumstances had thrown us together.''

''Circumstances didn't throw us together, you threw us together.''

''I, uh, it wasn't exactly like that.''

''Then why do you insist on sleeping with me every night?''

He ran a hand through his hair in vexation, then tried again to explain. ''Because I wanted you to want me. But I don't want you to do something you'll regret later, and—''

''Gavin? Shut up.'' She went up on tiptoe to kiss him, and his lungs shut down. He was already hard, had been hard since she'd mentioned the damn bed, and the feel of her soft body shifting against his as her warm tongue stroked into his mouth nearly buckled his knees.

Pulling away a scant inch, she drew a deep, shaky breath, then swallowed. Her eyes still held his, and her tone was a husky, warning growl. ''The only regrets will be yours when I murder you for being a tease. Please. Make love to me.''

Gavin stared a moment, stunned by her blunt plea. "Now?" *Please, let her mean now.*

Without looking away, Sara slammed and locked the front door. "Right now."

His breath left him in a loud whoosh. He trembled. He shifted. He grinned. "Okay, woman, you've convinced me." Gavin grabbed her hand and started down the hall at a trot.

And as he tugged her down onto the bed, his body covering her, she groaned in relief. "It's about time."

# 8

SARA CURLED INTO GAVIN, feeling his heat, his hardness. His mouth was hungry on hers, his breath coming fast and uneven. His hands seemed to be everywhere at once, but it wasn't enough. She clutched at his back, holding on as he rolled on the bed, positioning her firmly beneath him, working himself between her thighs, thrusting against her.

His hands slid down to her hips and his fingers dug into her flesh. He panted in excitement. "I'm sorry, Sara. Too fast."

"No!" She was so afraid he'd draw back, quit again, that she wrapped her legs around him. "Stay with me, Gavin."

"Oh, I intend to." But he pried himself loose, pinning her arms over her head and levering himself upward. "We have to slow down. I don't have any protection in here and..." His head fell forward and he groaned.

"Gavin?"

"Don't move, sweetheart. I swear. This time I'll be right back. Don't you dare move." He shoved himself off the bed and jogged out of the room.

Sara lay there staring at the ceiling. One. Two. Three. Four… Gavin was back. He set a box of condoms on the nightstand then turned to look at her. She remained perfectly still.

Fascinated, she watched his gaze going over her from her tangled hair to her feet. One of her sandals had fallen off, the other dangled from her toes. They had taken turns showering after his family arrived, and they were both dressed casually in shorts and T-shirts, but now Sara's shirt bunched up beneath her breasts and her shorts were unsnapped.

Gavin knelt on the bed, one large, hot hand coming to rest on her bare midriff. He stroked her, his hand trembling, his nostrils flaring as he struggled for breath. When he began slowly lowering her zipper, she brought her hands down to help him.

"No." Gavin caught her wrists and returned her arms to rest over her head. "Don't move. I mean it, Sara. You move and I'm done for."

"I can't just…"

"Yes, you can." He sounded very positive.

Then he caught her T-shirt and pulled it up until he could twist it around her wrists. He held it there with one hand while he deftly unhooked the front closure on her bra. The material parted and her breasts were exposed, her nipples tight, a light flush heating her skin.

Gavin stared, then closed his eyes with a guttural groan. ''Don't move.''

''You already said that.''

''I know.''

He went back to her shorts and Sara, though more excited than she'd ever thought imaginable, had to fight her embarrassment. ''I had no idea you were so kinky, Gavin.''

''This isn't kinky, babe. It's survival. I've wanted you for so damn long I can't remember not wanting you. And I've been disgustingly celibate for too many months. I'm working on a hair-trigger libido here. One wrong move, and…''

Stunned by his admission, Sara forgot to be embarrassed as he stripped her shorts down her legs and removed her one remaining sandal. She hadn't been with anyone, but then, there was no one she'd wanted. She'd never considered that Gavin had remained alone, too, since his breakup. She was amazed, and for the first time, she started to believe how much he might care for her. It seemed *un*believable, but also undeniable.

He traced his finger along the edge of her silky panties. Her breath constricted, her stomach muscles tightened. "Gavin? You've…you've really been celibate?"

"As chaste as a schoolgirl." His hot, intense gaze swept up her body, then settled on her face. "I didn't want anyone but you. Even before I broke things off with Karen, I was waiting for you. Just you, Sara."

Sara smiled, feeling oddly touched. She didn't know what to say, so she mumbled, "That's so sweet."

Gavin wasn't amused. He yanked her panties down, causing Sara to yelp. But before she could move he was over her, his mouth covering hers again, his tongue sliding in, hot and wet. His large palm smoothed over her breasts, pausing to lightly abrade her peaked nipples, then coasting down her belly and cupping over her mound.

"This is sweet, Sara." His fingers pushed inside her and she groaned. "Oh, yeah, very sweet."

For long, agonizing minutes Gavin tormented her. He wouldn't let her touch him at all, and that frustrated her. But how could she protest while he was making her squirm and beg and pant?

Gavin's mouth slid over her throat to her shoulder and then to her breast. He gently sucked her taut nipple into the heat of his mouth, and Sara felt her entire body clench. His fingers were still stroking over her, inside her, and she felt a wave of sizzling sensation begin. She fought it, but Gavin was relentless.

"Yes, honey." His tone was low and guttural, insistent. "Don't fight me, Sara. Not now."

Since she seemed to have very little choice in the matter, Sara gave in. Her climax was blinding, and she arched and twisted, hearing in the back of her mind all the soft, sultry words Gavin uttered to encourage her.

Limp, Sara was only vaguely aware of Gavin standing beside the bed removing his clothes. She opened her eyes a crack and surveyed his body. "That wasn't fair."

"Who ever told you love was fair?"

*Love?* Her heart skipped a beat and her emotions shattered. She didn't know if it was hope or fear or relief she felt, and since Gavin continued disrobing, she decided not to dwell on it. More than likely, it amounted to mere pillow talk. She wasn't overly familiar with the type of conversation appropriate at such a cataclysmic time.

Gavin's body demanded her attention, and her eyes widened as he shucked his shorts down his legs, taking off his underwear at the same time. She was sated, but she'd have to be dead not to be moved by such a sight. He was strong and powerful and pulsing with arousal. She could have looked at him all day and been deliriously happy. But Gavin wasn't very accommodating. He faced her, his hands fisted at his sides, and gave her only a scant second to soak in the sight of his nude perfection before he climbed back into bed with her and reached for the condoms.

"Let me," Sara said.

But Gavin gave her a horrified look. "Not on your life. I'd never live through it."

"I wouldn't hurt you."

"No, you'd kill me." She frowned and he added, "I mean it, Sara. You keep those little hands to yourself. Maybe later, after the box is nearly empty, I'll let you play touchy-feely. But not right now."

He seemed so serious, she couldn't help but chuckle. "So you can play, but I can't?"

"Damn right." He slid the condom on, then

turned toward her. ''I'm sorry, babe, but I'm short on control right now.''

''Then I'll hold you to your promise of later. Because I really am looking forward to touching you, Gavin.''

His expression stilled with her words, his chest heaving, his jaw tight, then he growled suddenly, ''Dammit!'' And Sara knew she'd said too much.

She loved his loss of control. Gavin was like a wild man, starving for her. And here she'd thought he didn't want her! Ha! She had wasted a lot of time, she decided.

But then she couldn't think anymore. Gavin pulled her legs apart and said in a rough whisper, ''Please tell me you're ready for me,'' and before she could answer, he pushed inside.

Frantically she tried to remind herself that sex was just sex, not love. But it didn't seem that way now. Not with Gavin staring down at her, his eyes so hot and filled with bursting emotion, his fingers twined with her own, gripping her, almost painful in their urgency.

''Sara,'' he breathed, and began to move.

Unbelievable the way the tension built again so soon. She cried out, but Gavin kissed her, his tongue deep in her mouth muffling the sound. When he came, he threw his head back and yelled like a crazy man. Sara touched him everywhere she could reach, stroking, kneading, then as he gave a great shudder she looked at his face and felt her own raging orgasm.

Very slowly, Gavin sank down onto her. She felt the harsh pounding of his heart against her breasts, felt his breath gusting against her sweat-damp skin as he tried to regulate his breathing. She was amazed. She was stunned.

Calm, confident, even-tempered Gavin was a wild man. Sara closed her eyes and hugged him close. She loved it.

MORNING SUN CAUSED his eyelids to twitch, and very warily, Gavin peered over at Sara. She was asleep, thank God. He felt numb all over, especially weak in the legs, and he wasn't certain he could do more than manage a shallow breath.

He'd planned, for so damn long, to make love with Sara and overwhelm her with his touted finesse.

Instead she'd damn near killed him.

She'd taken him seriously when he'd carried in the box of condoms. There couldn't be many left, probably only the ones he'd thrown beneath the bed, hiding them from her so she'd give him some rest. The little witch had been voracious. She certainly had more faith in his stamina than was warranted.

Many times he'd drifted into a deep sleep, only to jerk awake moments later, already hard, with her small hand stroking him or her mouth teasing him, or... But it had been wonderful. Exhausting, but wonderful. He muttered a quiet curse when he realized he was hard yet again.

He glanced at Sara's sprawled body and knew escape to be his only option. He had an hour before he needed to be on a job, and Sara had to go into work today, too. He sincerely hoped she had more energy than he did. His knees shook when he stood.

Satan and Tripod came together to the bedroom door when Gavin started out. The two pets had made a vicious ruckus last night when he and Sara had forgotten to let them back in. It had been the only reprieve Sara had given him, allowing him to feed the animals in the kitchen. But once that was done, Gavin found himself dragged back to the bedroom.

He grinned and shook his head. It hadn't taken Sara long at all to lose her inhibitions, and she was a glorious sight when she became demanding. He'd gladly play her sex slave again, just as soon as he had recuperated.

Picking up Satan and whistling softly to Tripod, he tiptoed out of the bedroom and into the hall, silently closing the door behind him. After giving the cat a few affectionate pats and rubbing Tripod behind the ears, he went into the bathroom to shower. He had just finished washing and was leaning back against the cool ceramic tile when the shower curtain opened and Sara stepped in. He gawked.

Sara slanted him a disgusted look, then stepped under the water. "Forget it, Gavin. I'm zonked."

Seeing that he was safe enough, he gave in to the urge to grin. She really did look exhausted, poor thing. He couldn't resist teasing her. "First wine, and now sex. You really do have this thing about overindulging, don't you?"

She pushed wet hair out of her face and glared at him. "Me? You're the one who wouldn't stop—"

"Oh, no, you don't. I was asleep, woman, and you—"

"You said I could touch you! But every single time I bumped you during the night you turned into a sex-crazed maniac!"

His fatigue miraculously disappeared while he watched the water sluice down her naked body. He picked up the soap and idly began working up a lather. "You have a way of *bumping* that sets a man off."

"*Everything* sets you off!"

"Well, what did you expect? I'd been deprived for too long. If you hadn't been so insistent on waiting…"

"Me!"

"Hush. Let me wash your back."

His hands went around her, then settled on her slick, wet skin. They smoothed over her shoulders, down the length of her spine, then lower. Sara said, "Gavin! That is not my back."

"That's okay." He kissed her throat, licking off a drop of water. "I dropped the soap anyway."

"Gavin…" Her voice dwindled to a throaty, demanding moan.

Twenty minutes later, they were both running late. Gavin finished dressing first, and he stopped on his way out the door to kiss Sara goodbye. She sat at the kitchen table, only half-dressed, still nursing a cup of coffee, and she barely managed a pucker.

He chuckled to himself as he headed for the office. He had papers to pick up, a few phone calls to make, he needed to meet the finishers at a house in less than an hour. His knees were shaky, his eyes burned from not enough sleep, and his heart felt full to bursting.

At this rate, Sara would cripple him within a week. But it was a week he anticipated with a good deal of excitement.

SHE WAS LATE, more than an hour and a half. Gavin was probably furious, since he had expected her home by six. Still, she sat in the car a few minutes longer, not opening the door, not looking at the house.

She heard the pitiful whining in the back seat and winced. Three pets was two more than Gavin had agreed to. Not that she felt she had to gain his permission for every little thing…but then, this wasn't a little thing. This was a very big thing. A very big, furry thing. With problems. *But what else could she have done?*

Sara saw the front door open, and then Gavin filled it. It was his habit to greet her at the front door each night after work, and she realized she'd already gotten used to it. He looked so good standing there, his hands on his hips, his brow furrowed in concern. He'd been worried about her? She hadn't considered that possibility. No one had worried about her in a very long time. He started down the steps, so she quickly came out of the car and met him on the sidewalk. She wrung her hands, trying to order her thoughts.

"Sara? What is it, what's the matter? Do you have any idea what time it is?"

His tone was sharp, a mixture of annoyance and worry. It was the first time he'd lost his temper with her since the day she'd brought home Tripod. She opened her mouth, ready to launch into her well-rehearsed explanations, and instead, she burst into tears. She was horrified by her own actions, but it had been such a horrendous afternoon.

Gavin grabbed her shoulders and shook her. "What the hell is the matter? Are you hurt? What happened?"

She shook her head, hiccuped, then tried again. "I'm sorry I'm late. I had to go by the shelter, and...Gavin, I have to tell you something."

He seemed to relax all at once. He pulled her close against his chest, and she didn't want to admit, even to herself, how wonderfully safe it felt. "Shh. Calm down, babe. Whatever it is, it'll be okay."

Then the sound of the sad, mournful whining reached their ears. Gavin froze for several heartbeats, then with a resigned sigh, he looked over her head to the car. Holding her shoulders, he pushed her back a ways to see her face. Sara bit her lip, knowing she looked guilty as sin, knowing she looked upset, but dammit all, there was nothing else she could have done. Gavin moved around her. Sara started talking ninety miles a minute. The problem was, she only had a fifty-mile-a-minute tongue, so most of what she said was garbled and nonsensical.

"It was the most terrible thing. Tragic. Just tragic. And so sad. You see, the old man died, and then the woman—his wife—just couldn't bear to go on without him, and she went into a decline. She's well over eighty, and she couldn't take care of herself, much less a dog. The family has its hands full looking after her, and the dog was simply wasting away. She misses everyone so much, and she's so unhappy. God, Gavin, I've never seen a more unhappy creature, and..."

Sara's explanation came to a screeching halt. Gavin opened the rear car door, shook his head, then began talking so softly, so calmly to the dog. When he lifted the collie out, holding her weight easily in his arms and started toward the house, Sara was speechless. She trotted after him.

"What are you doing?"

Gavin never slowed his pace. He crooned to the dog, but he turned his head enough to say, "She's upset. I'm taking her inside.'' The dog looked up at him, and Gavin asked, ''What's her name?''

''Maggie.''

He said the name, softly, slowly, making it sound like a compliment, and the dog stared at him as if captivated. Sara stepped through the doorway, holding the door for Gavin, and Satan and Tripod walked to her with rapt looks of curiosity. She took a brief moment to pat the animals, then rushed after Gavin. He took the dog to the kitchen and sat her on the floor by the sink, in the spot where the late-day sun coming through the window made a warm, golden pool on the tile.

Gavin knelt in front of Maggie, rubbing her laid-back ears. Maggie curled into a small semicircle, her entire countenance one of wary disbelief. ''What's the matter, old girl? This is all pretty new, isn't it? But you're okay here.''

His understanding, the gentle tone of his voice, brought on a fresh rush of tears. Sara felt her bottom lip begin to quiver and pulled it tightly between her teeth. Tripod sat back to watch the happenings from a distance, choosing to lean against Sara's leg. But Satan observed the situation with a jaundiced eye, then walked over and regally placed himself over Gavin's knee. The look he gave the dog was filled with possessive warning. Gavin chuckled, stroking the cat.

"Be nice now, Satan. You can see she's scared. Make her welcome."

Satan blinked, gave one of his rumbling, rusty purrs, and brushed against the dog. The dog's head snapped back as if startled, but Satan was relentless. Within moments, Maggie was splotched with Satan's yellow hair. But she didn't seem to mind, especially since Gavin was still petting her. Tripod moved closer and sniffed the dog, then flopped down beside her. She looked ready to go to sleep.

Sara sniffled, so touched by the scene she could barely keep her tears in check. Gavin heard the small sound and turned to her. "Why don't you go take your bath, honey? I'll look after Maggie, get her settled down for the night. In the morning, she'll feel better."

That did it. Sara wailed, covering her face with her hands. Only a second later, she felt Gavin pull her close. "Shh. It's all right now."

"I... I...know." She hiccuped, then made an effort to calm herself, but it was impossible. "I didn't know what to do. When Jess called me at work to tell me about Maggie, I just had to go and see her for myself. She wouldn't eat and she kept whimpering and she...well, she was so alone. So scared. You can't imagine what that's like, Gavin."

"Shh. It's all right now."

"I just had to bring her home."

"Of course you did. And now she'll feel loved again and everything will be fine."

After a loud, disgusting sniff, Sara wiped her eyes with the back of her hand. It was then she realized the kitchen smelled of cooked chicken. She looked around and saw a variety of pots and pans on the stove, and the table was set, complete with a lit candle. Or at least, it had been lit some time ago. The wick had long since burned down. Oh, no. Gavin had cooked dinner and she'd missed it. Again. He'd wasted another special meal on her.

"I'm so sorry." She wiped her eyes again, trying to rid herself of the insistent tears. She put her hands on his chest and looked up at him. "You went to all this trouble, and I wasn't even here in time to appreciate it."

After a long, intense look, Gavin glanced over his shoulder to where Maggie was allowing Satan to curl into her side. The dog gave a single, loving lick to the cat, leaving Satan's entire head damp and his fur ruffed in the wrong direction. Satan closed his eyes and rumbled a ragged purr. Tripod never stirred. Gavin turned back to Sara and kissed her. "I'd say you were doing something more important. And dinner isn't wasted. We can eat the chicken cold. In fact, take your bath and I'll set us up a picnic outside. The animals could use the night air."

Suddenly she couldn't breathe. Sara took a step back, appalled, frightened, amazed. It wasn't a slow awareness, but a burst of realization that nearly brought her to her knees. *She loved him.* She didn't want to, didn't want to set herself up for another disappointment, another hurt. But he gave her no choice, damn him. How could she not love a man who'd put the needs of an animal above his own?

The words felt choked as she forced them through her throat. "Why are you doing this?"

Gavin knelt again by Maggie's side and stroked along her back. This time the dog lifted her tail in a one-thump wag.

Gavin seemed to take an inordinate amount of time before answering. Finally he looked up, his expression blank of all emotion. "Did you really expect me to play the tyrant and demand you take the dog back? Only a real bastard would refuse to give that dog a little love. Ah, and you were late, too. Should I have thrown a tantrum because dinner was ruined? Would you have dealt better with that?''

Sara shook her head, even as she said, ''I don't know.''

''You don't know me. Yet you keep comparing me to Ted and your parents and every other person who ever let you down, and I don't mind telling you, it makes me mad as hell.''

''I didn't—''

''Yes, you did. Why would you think I'd feel any less compassion for that dog than you do?''

''Because...'' Sara swallowed. She drew in a ragged breath and started again. ''Because you don't know what it means to be alone and scared and—'' Her voice broke, but Gavin didn't make a move toward her. He continued to stroke the dog, and occasionally Satan when the cat demanded it. But his gaze never left her face, and through her tears, Sara saw his understanding. It was humiliating, because she had a feeling he knew her better than she knew herself.

''I'm going to go take my bath now.''

Gavin nodded. ''I'll get our dinner together. And Sara? When we're done eating, we're going to talk.''

It sounded closer to a threat than a mere statement. Gavin watched her closely, as did Satan and Maggie. Even Tripod managed to stir herself enough to give a quick glance. Sara felt outnumbered, and after a huge sigh, she nodded agreement.

As if relieved by Sara's decision, Maggie laid her head on Gavin's thigh. The dog no longer looked so cautious or forlorn. And Satan seemed to be taking the addition of yet another pet in stride. That is, until he stood up and decided to mark Gavin as his own territory in the time-honored tradition of all male animals. Gavin jumped to his feet, but not in time.

Sara realized she no longer felt like crying. In fact, she had to hold her mouth to stifle her laughter. She had just turned to leave the kitchen when she heard Gavin mutter, "I'll put ten bows on you, dammit! Do I *look* like a tree?''

# 9

FOR MOST OF HER LIFE, Sara had felt hollow. She hadn't realized that until now, when she felt ready to burst with an incredible wealth of emotion. She'd lived with emptiness so long, it was almost alarming to acknowledge the difference now. But feelings she'd never encountered before filled her, making her whole. She wanted to cry, she wanted to laugh.

She wanted to tell Gavin that she loved him.

But she didn't dare.

This was all too new and too fragile to put to the test so soon. As she sat through the dinner that Gavin had prepared, on the tablecloth he'd spread on the ground, she couldn't help but smile. He coddled Maggie, he calmed Tripod and he reassured Satan, all without thought. Simply because he was that kind of man—so different from any other person she'd ever known.

That, too, was frightening. How could a man like Gavin ever really care about her? She was so used to people turning away, or in Ted's case, running away. She wanted to surround herself with things that would be permanent. Like her house, her pets. But she couldn't make Gavin permanent. He would only stay if he chose to.

He looked up and caught her staring. She smiled, a sappy smile, she knew. Then she leaned over the food and kissed him. "Thank you."

He didn't question her sudden gratitude, or want an explanation for what she was thankful for. He merely nodded. "You're welcome."

"You're too good to me."

Gavin shot her a look, growled low enough to startle all three animals, then hauled Sara over the food, scattering plates and chicken and knocking over drinks. She found herself facedown over his lap, with his hand hovering over her backside.

"Gavin! What in the world…"

"What did you say, Sara?"

"Uh…" She wasn't certain what had prompted this barbarian mood of his, so she didn't know how to answer. But she did giggle.

His palm thwacked lightly on her upturned derriere. She tried, but couldn't quite stifle another giggle.

"That was what I wanted to talk to you about."

"My backside?"

"No, this damn habit you have of thinking I'm being too good to you."

"Oh." Her tone softened. "You really are— Ouch!"

"Did that sting?"

"You don't sound the least bit remorseful." She tried to rub her bottom, but he caught her hands and held them away.

"I'm not remorseful. Now let's try this again. Repeat after me."

"Yes, sir." She started to giggle again. She doubted, in her present mood and her newly acknowledged love, that Gavin could do anything to dampen her spirits or make her angry.

"Say, I deserve the very best there is."

"You are that, Gavin."

"My palm is itching, Sara. I think I may have a propensity for this type of thing. Don't tempt me."

"I deserve the very best."

"Much better." He began to massage her bottom. "Now say, I will stop keeping track of every nice thing Gavin does and accept his affection without remorse."

His roving, caressing hand made speech difficult. Sara squirmed over his knees. "Yeah, what you said."

"I want you to be happy, Sara."

All the teasing had gone out of his tone. When she tried to turn over, he helped her until she was cradled in his arms. She kissed his chin, his cheek. "I *am* happy. Very happy." She kissed his mouth, and the next thing she knew, she was lying on her back on the soft grass, with Gavin's weight pressing into her.

"You make me happy, too, babe. Believe that, will you?"

She didn't answer him. He didn't give her a chance to.

HE WAS READY TO KILL HER.

One animal had been enough. Two, he could have tolerated. Even three, given the circumstances, he'd have handled just fine. But five? He stared at the old, shivering poodle she held in her arms and felt his temper ready to snap.

"What's the matter with this one?"

Sara flinched slightly, and she had a little trouble meeting his direct gaze, but she finally muttered, "He's deaf."

Deaf. A deaf poodle. Just ducky. "Sara, I thought we agreed after the last dog—"

"I had to bring Melon home! No one would

have wanted a pregnant dog. After she has her puppies, we'll find a home for them."

"And for this...this decrepit old soul? You know you won't want to part with any of them, Sara."

She hugged the poodle closer to her chest. "It's a good thing he can't hear you. And he's not decrepit. Just a little..."

"Ancient? Hell, I see gray hairs on him."

"That's the natural color of his coat."

"Yeah, right. What about his double chin? I swear, I've never seen a dog with a double chin before."

"He needs to be treated gently."

That was the thing about Sara. She seemed to have taken his words to heart two weeks ago. She was more relaxed around him, more accepting of him. But she still wanted to save every single animal that came into the shelter. Luckily the backyard held up, but they had to take regular duty with the scooper twice a day, and the pet-food bill grew daily. Gavin honestly hated to stem her enthusiasm for helping the animals, but enough was enough.

"Sara, this is not a halfway house for socially challenged animals. The last two you brought home weren't at the shelter long enough to be adopted.''

''Because I know whoever took them wouldn't have been as good to them as we are.'' The poodle lifted his grizzled head and gave Sara a slow lick on the chin. Gavin winced.

''Babe, listen to reason. When Melon has her pups we're going to be overrun with dogs. Poor Satan is liable to run away, Tripod will go into a nervous decline, Maggie will hide—''

He stopped abruptly when the poodle turned watery eyes in his direction, looking wounded to his very soul.

*Dammit all.*

He fought the inevitable for another three seconds, then stomped forward. ''Here, give him to me. He's probably cold, even as warm as it is. I'll put him in on Maggie's blanket.''

Sara's grateful smile wobbled. ''Thank you.''

Gavin managed to point an accusing finger, and his frown was downright mean. ''That's enough out of you, lady.''

She took his warning to heart and turned away, but he still caught sight of her smile. She trusted him now. But she still hadn't told him she cared.

He was about at the end of his patience.

After getting all the animals settled, Gavin located Sara in the laundry room and announced he had work to do. "The finishers are still up at the house. I want to go check on them, make certain they're on schedule. Tomorrow we'll be getting a new shipment of drywall and now that three of the houses are almost complete, I don't want to fall behind."

"It will be strange having neighbors, won't it?"

Gavin grinned. He knew Sara liked having the street to themselves, but she was also extremely proud every time he sold a house. So far, all the lots had been taken, with plans for the house styles already chosen. Within a year, all the buildings would be complete, and the street would become a neighborhood. Maybe, Gavin thought, someone moving in would want a dog.

He gave Sara a quick kiss. "We'll eat out tonight, okay?"

"I could cook if you want."

*"No."* He hoped he hadn't sounded too anxious, but in truth, Sara's cooking was almost inedible. "We deserve a night out."

"All right. I'll have all the housework done before you get home."

She was always so eager to please him, working extra hard to uphold her end of their bargain

of sharing the chores. He shook his head, knowing
better than to argue with her again. She was ad-
amant that she always do her share. She worked
so hard at making the relationship work, but she
never gave him what he really wanted—a declaration of love.

SARA HURRIED THROUGH the house, making certain everything was tidy, sparing herself enough
time to get ready for dinner. She wanted to look
extra nice tonight, since Gavin was taking her out.
She did her best never to look frumpy around him,
though there wasn't anything she could do about
her hair, which would always have a tendency to
go its own way, regardless of her coercion. Gavin
had told her once that he liked it for that very
reason.

She was dabbing on a touch of makeup when
the doorbell rang and all four dogs began barking
at once. She had to shove animals aside to reach
the doorknob, and when she opened it, she wished
she hadn't bothered.

Her ex-fiancé, Ted, stood on the front porch,
his hands shoved into his pockets, a suave smile
on his handsome face. She took two steps back.

Her simple movement jump-started the outraged barking. All the animals seemed to vie for

the greatest show of bluster, growling and snarling and forcing the hair on their backs to stand up. All but the poodle, who couldn't get his hair to oblige. But he made up for it by taking small, snapping bites of the air very near to Ted's leg.

"What the hell! Where did you get all these creatures?"

Sara had her hands full trying to calm the animals. "These are my pets. Hush, dogs!" They ignored her. While they had each openly accepted Gavin, not a single one of them seemed inclined to allow Ted past the front door.

Except for Satan.

Satan just sat and watched from a padded chair arm, his round eyes unblinking, his expression suspicious.

Ted tried to shout over the noise. "I'd like to talk to you, honey."

"I'm not your honey." Sara made a grab for Maggie, who was behaving in a very un-Maggielike manner. She caught the dog's collar and began dragging her toward the kitchen, at the same time urging Tripod forward with the edge of her shoe. Ted stepped inside and stared.

"My God. That dog's missing a leg."

She ignored him and whistled for Melon, the only one of the bunch who would respond to such a command. The heavily pregnant animal lumbered behind, but she kept looking over her shoulder and growling at Ted. Since Melon was a singularly ugly bulldog, it was a sight to cause awe.

Ted called out, "The damn poodle is still threatening to bite me. Whistle for it."

"Won't do me any good," Sara yelled between bouts of barking. "He's deaf. Can't hear me anyway."

Ted stared at her in amazement. Then his expression suddenly softened. "My poor baby."

Sara closed the low gate to the kitchen and admonished the dogs to quiet down. Gavin had purchased the spring-action gate after having a night with Sara interrupted. Tripod and Maggie had decided to sleep with them, and Satan, of course, had refused to be left out. In truth, Sara wondered if Satan might not have led the troop.

She picked up the poodle and set him gently over the gate then turned back to Ted. "Now, what exactly did you need, Ted?"

He maintained his tender expression and pronounced, "You. I need you, Sara. And obviously you need me, too."

Sara stared. "What in the world are you blathering about?"

"It's plain to see, sweetheart." He shook his

head in a pitying way and smiled again. "You're surrounding yourself by these pathetic creatures because you miss me. You need to be loved."

Sara felt as if someone had poleaxed her. *She needed to be loved?* It wasn't just permanency she craved? No, of course not. She did want to be loved. She wanted that so desperately, she'd been afraid to admit it, even to herself. She'd been doubly afraid to admit it to Gavin.

Then she stiffened her spine. No more. She wouldn't remain a coward. She loved Gavin and he deserved the truth, despite what his reaction might be. If he didn't care enough about her, if he couldn't learn to love her, then he might want to go now before her feelings began to suffocate him.

Sara paced. How to tell him? She couldn't very well just blurt it out...

Ted cleared his throat. "Sara?"

She glanced up, surprised to see Ted still standing there. He moved closer, and all the animals were quiet, as if waiting. Sara blinked at him in question.

"I'm sorry I hurt you, sweetheart. It was never my intention."

"No? That's strange. Did you honestly think I

would appreciate having my fiancé in my bed with my neighbor's girlfriend?''

Ted made a *tsking* sound. ''It wasn't exactly like that, Sara. I just got carried away. We both did. But we realize now what we might have thrown away by acting so—''

''We?'' Sara felt her insides freeze, her lungs constrict. Ted took a step closer. Satan made an agile leap from the chair and sauntered slowly toward them.

''Karen and I.'' Ted glanced at the cat, then back to Sara's face. ''I want to make it up to you, Sara. I want to come back to you.''

A bubble of laughter took her by surprise. ''That's absurd.'' She flapped her hand, dismissing the mere suggestion of such a ridiculous thing, then asked, ''Did you say, Karen? She's here?''

''Yes, of course.'' This obviously wasn't going the way Ted had intended. ''Listen to me, Sara. We can make a go of things. I'm ready now.''

''I'm not.'' She forcibly kept her tone one of polite inquiry. ''Where, exactly, is Karen?''

He heaved an impatient breath. ''She went up to the empty house that worker boyfriend of hers is at. She saw him go inside the garage just as we turned on the street. She's hoping to patch things up with him.''

Sara felt every protective, possessive instinct she owned come slamming to the surface. Karen with Gavin? Beautiful, tall, sexy Karen. Good grief.

She started to move around Ted, her steps anxious. "Excuse me, I have to go."

Ted turned, startled. "Go where?"

"After Gavin."

"Who the hell is Gavin?"

"The man you'll never be. Let yourself out, will you?"

"Now, wait a damn minute!"

With his raised tone, all the dogs howled in outrage. They leaned against the gate, snarling and yapping and doing their best to get through. Sara tried to ignore them all; her only thought was to get to Gavin and tell him her feelings before Karen had a chance to work on him. Not that she didn't trust Gavin, but this was too important to leave to chance.

But then Ted stupidly grabbed her arm to halt her exit, and all hell broke loose.

Satan roared out the most ferocious, menacing, hair-raising growl Sara had ever heard from him, and the gate in the kitchen collapsed from the combined weights of four enraged dogs. Ted flew from the house, high-pitched screams of fright signaling his terror. The animals took off in furious pursuit, Satan leading the way.

Sara watched it all in mingled amazement and horror, then she remembered Gavin. And Karen. And her love.

She thundered after the group, every step echoing her resolve.

GAVIN DID HIS BEST to free himself from Karen's grasping hold. The woman had no shame, especially given they were standing in the open garage. Twice now he'd told her it was over, that he'd meant it when he'd broken things off so long ago. Even without Sara in his life, he wouldn't take Karen back. She wasn't the type of woman he wanted or needed to be with.

He tried to be gentle, but Karen was deliberately obstinate about the whole thing. She refused to listen.

Gavin sighed in disgust as she once again threw herself against his chest and wrapped her arms around him. He propped his hands on his hips, allowing her, for the moment, to have her say. It wouldn't matter. He wanted Sara, and he'd have her eventually on his terms, no matter how long he had to wait, or how many pets he had to put up with. Sooner or later the woman would realize she loved him.

He could feel Karen cuddling closer and once again he clamped his hands on her forearms and prepared to pry her loose. Then they heard the noise.

Karen looked up just as Gavin leaned around her.

Racing down the middle of the street, looking much like a bizarre circus parade, was Sara's ex-fiancé Ted and every pet Gavin had recently acquired. They made a huge amount of noise—a mixture of human horror and animal determination. Gavin started to chuckle.

Good old Satan led the group, galloping at full speed, his heavy body stiff with anger, his bent tail sticking out like a broken lance. All the dogs followed, even the aged poodle. As Gavin watched, Ted made a leap for a skinny little tree and hoisted himself upward.

Satan followed.

Ted wailed as the cat perched on the same branch, then sat back to watch. The cat didn't make another move, but he looked down at the loudly yapping dogs with faint approval.

Sara appeared.

She took one look at Karen draped in Gavin's

arms and began a forceful, determined stride in their direction. She was breathing hard, and she looked as enraged as the animals.

Karen stiffened. "Oh my God."

Gavin allowed her to jump behind him and use him as a shield. Sara looked ready to explode with righteous anger. Gavin couldn't have been more pleased. There was no way he could mistake the jealousy in her eyes. Her lips were pulled back in a snarl and he could just see the tip of her crooked tooth.

He wanted very badly to kiss her.

When Sara got close enough, he grinned and reached into the garage for the plastic rake leaning against the wall, then offered it to her with a flourish. It was a subtle reminder, giving Sara the chance to collect herself before she did something she might regret later.

To his surprise she smiled, but it was a smile with evil intent. "I love you, Gavin."

For a long moment he couldn't move. Hell, he could barely breathe. Sara looked so stern, so forbidding. Her arms were held stiff at her sides, the rake in one fist, her legs braced apart. She'd said it like a command, and he nodded. "It's about damn time."

She took a step back, stunned. "Then I don't need the rake?"

"You don't need the rake."

She glanced at Karen who dared to peek over his shoulder. "You have about three seconds to make yourself scarce before I sic the animals on you."

Karen screamed, causing Gavin's ears to ring, and then she ran. Gavin started laughing and couldn't stop. Ted hollered for someone to help.

He and Sara both ignored him.

After fidgeting a moment, Sara took a small step closer. "I've been afraid to tell you."

"I know." Overwhelmed by tenderness Gavin touched her cheek. "I would have waited awhile longer before getting insistent."

"Insistent about what?"

"About hearing a declaration. About getting married." He didn't like his own feeling of insecurity, but he acknowledged it. "You will marry me, won't you?"

"I'll insist upon it."

Gavin pulled her close and began kissing her. It was only the honking of horns that forced him to pull away. "Oh, hell."

Sara followed his line of vision and then

blinked in surprise. "Your family's coming to visit again?"

"Sort of. You see, you mentioned to Mom that you needed lawn furniture. That's probably what's in the truck."

Sara was stunned. "I can't accept lawn furniture from her!"

"Trust me, honey. She likes giving things. The whole family does. Do you think you'll mind being married to the spoiled, youngest child of the family?"

She gave him a slow, blinding smile that nearly melted his heart. "Are you kidding? I get you and lawn furniture? What more could any woman possibly want?"

# *Epilogue*

THEY ANNOUNCED THEIR intent to marry an hour later over coffee and cookies. It hadn't been easy to explain Ted, especially since he'd refused to come out of the tree. When he did come down, he had no way to leave; Karen had taken the car.

Gavin called for a cab, then explained to everyone that Ted preferred to wait on the curb—with Satan—until the cab arrived. Not a soul questioned that decision.

Sara had even more relatives to meet this time. It seemed his mother thought Gavin could use the extra support of the elders in the family, so there were two sets of grandparents tagging along. When the oldsters discovered Gavin had managed quite nicely on his own, they each claimed good genes as the deciding factor in his victory.

After Ted was finally picked up, the animals all wandered back to the house. Sara retold the story of how the pets had rallied together to come to her defense, and everyone was suitably impressed.

Grandpa Blake showed a special fondness for the sweet-tempered Maggie. He claimed to have had a dog just like her in his youth.

Gavin's grandmother on his mother's side ended up with Tripod in her lap, throughout the entire visit praising the animal for her courage. And as Gavin watched them all interact, an idea came to mind.

"Does the retirement village allow you to have pets, Grandpa?"

"They do, and I know a lot of the folks in the village would love to have a good, dedicated dog. But most of them are on limited incomes and pets cost money."

Sara picked up on Gavin's train of thought immediately. "I have two friends who run a shelter. I bet they'd be willing to give the shots and checkups for free if the animals had a good place to stay. And Gavin and I could build a run of sorts right off the back door of each condo, so all the owner would have to do is hook the dog to a leash in the morning."

Gavin nodded. "It could be done. The village is set up with only ground-floor condos. If Jess and Lou would agree…"

"I'm certain they would." Sara looked so excited by the idea, Gavin knew she would be comfortable with the animals' living arrangements. They could personally select which homes the dogs and cats would go to.

All the elders agreed to take a pet from the shelter. They even seemed anxious about the idea. Sara promised to go first thing the next day and see what animals were available.

Gavin bided his time until he could get Sara alone in the kitchen for a few minutes, and then he pulled her close. She snuggled into him with a sigh of pleasure. "Thank you for coming up with such a wonderful plan, Gavin. It makes me so happy to know that a lot of the animals won't have to be alone anymore."

He squeezed her a little tighter. "They remind you of how you've felt for much of your life."

She nodded, then laid her cheek against his chest. "But at least I understand that now. And I think, if you don't mind, I'll try inviting my parents to the wedding."

"Of course I don't mind. Why don't we drive over and see them together? We can ask in person. You said they didn't live all that far away."

"Not too far." She stared up at him and sighed in wonder. "I really do love you, you know."

And he did know. He'd known all along she

could give him what no other woman could. Herself.

He was just about to kiss her when he heard the rushing steps of a small army of children. They squealed in delight as they raced past Gavin and Sara in the kitchen, Satan hot on their heels. And as the cat flew past in graceful, playful pursuit, he looked up, and Gavin could have sworn he was grinning.

Sara laughed. ''Your mother's right. He's just like you.''

Gavin merely grinned.

**Modern Romance**™
...seduction and
passion guaranteed

**Tender Romance**™
...love affairs that
last a lifetime

**Sensual Romance**™
...sassy, sexy and
seductive

*Blaze*
...sultry days and
steamy nights

**Medical Romance**™
...medical drama on
the pulse

**Historical Romance**™
...rich, vivid and
passionate

*29 new titles every month.*

*With all kinds of Romance for
every kind of mood...*

MILLS & BOON®

*Makes any time special*™

MAT4

# 2 FREE

## books and a surprise gift!

We would like to take this opportunity to thank you for reading this Mills & Boon® book by offering you the chance to take TWO more specially selected titles from the Sensual Romance™ series absolutely FREE! We're also making this offer to introduce you to the benefits of the Reader Service™—

- ★ FREE home delivery
- ★ FREE gifts and competitions
- ★ FREE monthly Newsletter
- ★ Exclusive Reader Service discounts
- ★ Books available before they're in the shops

Accepting these FREE books and gift places you under no obligation to buy, you may cancel at any time, even after receiving your free shipment. Simply complete your details below and return the entire page to the address below. *You don't even need a stamp!*

**YES!** Please send me 2 free Sensual Romance books and a surprise gift. I understand that unless you hear from me, I will receive 4 superb new titles every month for just £2.49 each, postage and packing free. I am under no obligation to purchase any books and may cancel my subscription at any time. The free books and gift will be mine to keep in any case.

T1ZEA

Ms/Mrs/Miss/Mr .............................Initials....................................
BLOCK CAPITALS PLEASE

Surname ....................................................................................................

Address ....................................................................................................

....................................................................................................................

....................................................Postcode....................................

**Send this whole page to:**
**UK: FREEPOST CN81, Croydon, CR9 3WZ**
**EIRE: PO Box 4546, Kilcock, County Kildare (stamp required)**